The Realmwalker Chronicles:

The Pillars of Natura

Volume 1: Maior

By Lee Aarons
Illustrations by Spenn

Author: Lee Aarons
Interior/Cover Art: Spenn
Maps: Stephen Lobbes
Cover Design: Matthew Porter
Editor: Stephanie Mitchell, Ph.D.

Printed in the United States of America
First Printing, 2014

ISBN 978-0615562162

Realmwalker Publishing Group, Inc.
13290 W. Mill Road
Malcolm, NE 68402

www.RealmwalkerPublishing.com

Ordering Information:
Quantity sales. Special discounts are available on quantity purchases by corporations, associations, and others. For details, contact the publisher at the address above.

Orders by U.S. trade bookstores and wholesalers. Please contact us:
Phone: (402) 450-6582
email: sales@realmwalkerpublishinggroup.com

The Realmwalker Chronicles

Book 1: The Pillars of Natura
Volume 1: Maior
Volume 2: Halen
Volume 3: D'Ware
Volume 4: Nym

Book 2: The Reign of Fire
Volume 5: Merlan
Volume 6: Djinn
Volume 7: Fon
Volume 8: Dragon

Book 3: The Machine of War
Volume 9: Degar
Volume 10: Sonnan
Volume 11: Oham
Volume 12: Sol

Book 4: The Dark Imaginings
Volume 13: Mala
Volume 14: Lyren
Volume 15: Yori
Volume 16: Reaver

Contents

Prologue: Breaking The Lion 1
Chapter 1: Upon This Rock 11
Chapter 2: To Save a Life 22
Chapter 3: Stir of Echoes 29
Chapter 4: A Fear and a Dread 38
Chapter 5: Decisions 49
Chapter 6: The Honor of One 57
Chapter 7: Behold My Children 65
Chapter 8: Through the Fire and Flames 74
Chapter 9: Manifestations 86
Chapter 10: RED 96
Chapter 11: First Night 111
Chapter 12: The Road to Jaske Green 120
Chapter 13: The Thunder Rolls 131

Maps & Illustrations

The Four Realms x
Map of Natura xi
Under the Dome 4
Map of Domo Vale Region 9
The Smoke's Embrace 31
Kanias Emerges 93

For my Grandfather, Lee Drake.
You taught me the power of words.

Acknowledgments

First of all I would like to thank my dear family. Specifically, my amazing mother, Madeline Drake, who has always been there for me. Everything that I know about perseverance, courage, hope and love, I have learned from her. Words will never say enough.

To my wife, Stephanie Mitchell, I can only say that without her love, tireless support, and superb editing skill, not only would this novel not be finished, but I would not be the person that I am today. She is my Sunshine.

I would also like to offer a special thank you to my good friend and creative partner, Seth Penn, whose hard work, boundless creativity, and dedication to his craft are what made this novel what you see today. His illustrations and enthusiasm breathed life into this project and it was my partnership with him that finally brought everything together.

I would be remiss not to mention our mutual friend, Melia Ptacek, who first brought Seth's talent to my attention. Our partnership is the direct result of her belief that our collaboration would bring out the best in both of us.

Finally, I would like to thank the countless others who have contributed to this work either by listening to my ideas (both good and bad), providing advice, inspiring me, or simply putting up with my silly obsession. There have been many starts and stops in my attempt to tell this story over the years with so many extraordinary people who have contributed and supported me along my journey. Unfortunately, due to my own hubris and habit of procrastination, many gave up hope that this project would ever be completed, including myself. Some have felt their support of me and of this project was in vain. It is my sincerest hope that having this book in their hands will, in some measure, help them feel vindicated, through the realization that their faith in me is at last rewarded with results.

The desire to tell this story may have been the impetus that ignited this labor of love, but my continuing motivation was found in my desire to honor everyone's past and present contributions. What you are about to read would have never come full circle without it.

The Four Realms of Erta
NATURA
Beings - Creatures - Plants - Time
ELEMENTA
Air - Fire - Stone - Water
NECRO
Disease - Shadow - Shape - Soul
MECHO
Charge - Light - Sound - Thermal

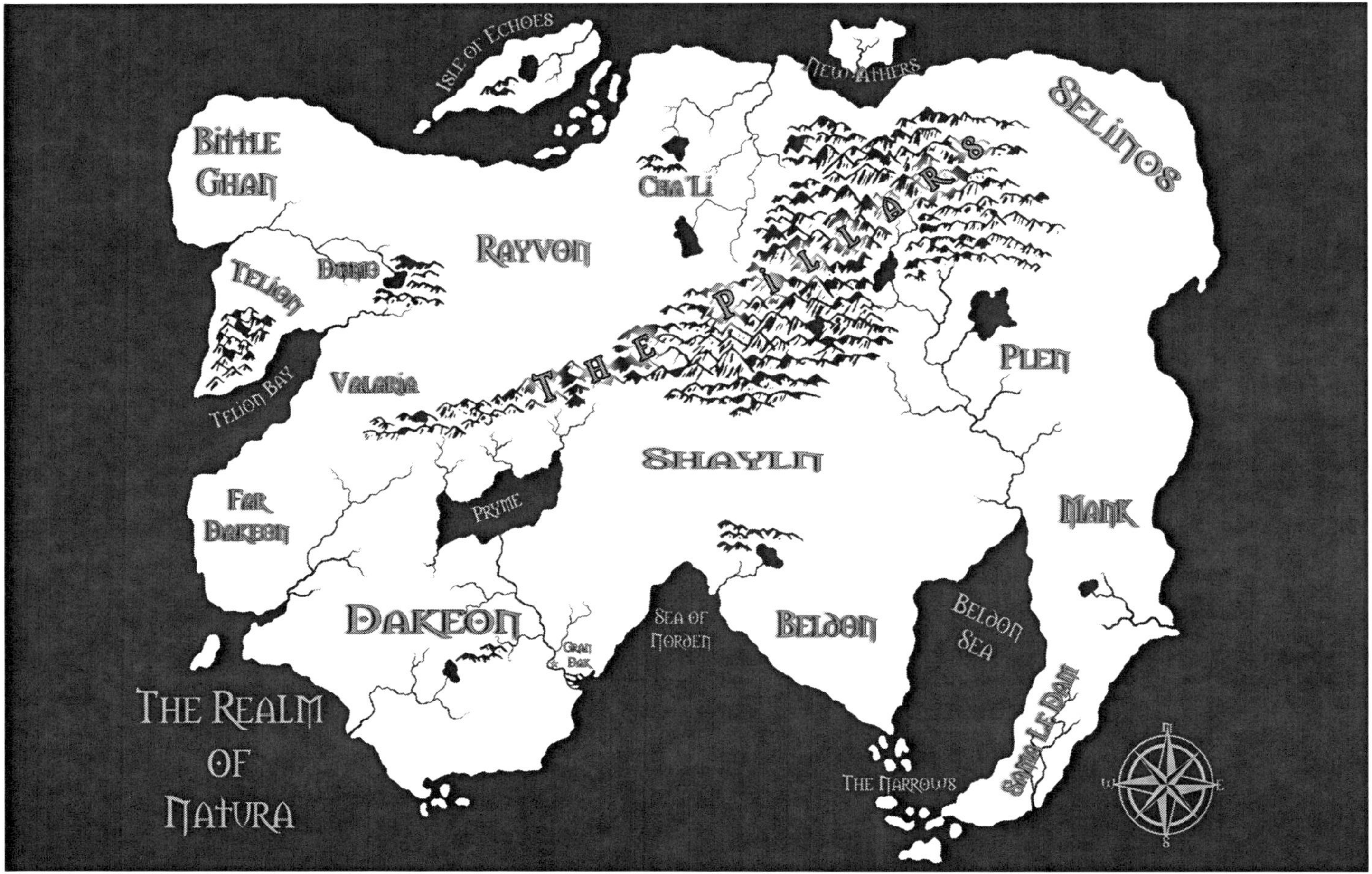

The Realm of Natura
Isle of Echoes
New Athers
Selinos
Bittle Ghan
Cha'Li
Rayvon
Telion
The Pillars
Plen
Valaria
Telion Bay
Shayln
Far Dakeon
Pryme
Mank
Dakeon
Gran Dak
Sea of Norden
Beldon
Beldon Sea
The Narrows

Prologue: Breaking the Lion

STANDING as if a mighty hand had simply pulled them from the ground, the great mountains rose abruptly from the pine-scented hills that lay before them, carrying the sky upon their broad snow-covered shoulders. The late day sun cast a warm golden glow upon the western slopes of the massive range, diffusing in the frosty alpine air. Flooding the deep valleys and bathing the high ridges, the light was full of lies. There was no evidence of warmth, only a promise of it, to be found within its beams.

Far up the slopes of Mount Chaldan, the highest peak, yet still far below the summit, the legendary Temple of Erta grew out of the mountain's face. The pinnacle of all things ever made by mortal hands in the Realm, it stood proudly, wearing the sunlight like a crown, its gleaming white buildings and high domes glittering in the failing light. The immense wall around it was built into the mountain itself, daring to separate all that was great from the mundane world. Spaced along the great barrier, four powerful towers rose up like giant sentinels, standing silently, watching the road wind like a brown ribbon from the valley to skirt their mighty feet before continuing its journey over the passes to the East.

Despite the beauty and grandeur, despite their attempts to

honor the majesty and grace of the Goddess Erta, they were all inferior testaments. In any other location in the Four Realms, perhaps they could have been seen with an unprejudiced eye. In this place, however, they lay in the shadow of divine proof, too easily humbled and dismissed by a true display of grandeur, the mountain range that Her own immortal hands had wrought on the Day of Creation: The Pillars of Natura.

As if realizing that the attempt to impress the great peaks had failed, the sunlight began to dim, twilight devouring the Temple's great structures with ravenous shadows of a night that would never fully come. In moments, the sun reached its lowest point in the sky, only a few weak rays touching upon the highest and most illustrious dome in the middle of the compound. Streaming in through a narrow window high upon the dome, the cold light cast a dim halo around the dying man within, the echoes of his latest screams fading into the shadows pressing in around him and the three bowed figures holding vigil at his bedside.

It will not be long now.

Ge'Lion's thoughts cleared as the motes of pain finally began to dissipate from his eyes. Reflexively, his fingers reached out, brushing the leather-wrapped hilt of the long sword laying at his side. He felt the familiar tug at the back of his mind. Even now, lying in his death bed, the Sword of Angios was part of him, touching his mind, feeding his Spirit, willing him to live, and compelling him to serve.

Angios can feel it, and so can I—Erta's need. Yet I am unable to answer the call. When will the Successor be found? Someone who can serve the Goddess and wield Angios after me? Erta needs Her new champion and my time is—

As if in response to his deepest concern, the man's thoughts were shattered by a storm of rending agony surging again through his once powerful body. His broad chest rose and fell unsteadily as his burning lungs snatched at elusive gulps of air between his screams.

Much too short.

He perceived the fear and resignation in the voices of the three Seraph attendants making petitions to Erta for Her healing and mercy as they knelt nearby.

Only three.

The fact that only three remained to watch over him told the story of their desperation. That three remained behind at all told the story of their respect. They would not permit their leader to die alone. Any hope they had however, was fading along with the light in the chamber, the darkness becoming a blanket of despair preparing to cover him for his final rest.

As he was about to surrender himself to that despair, bringing his misery to an end, Ge'Lion began gasping again, his thoughts shattering anew. This time, however, it was not bone deep agony that sent him reeling. This new shock was from an overwhelming surge of power from Angios. It mingled with the fading remnants of his own fortitude, coursing through him and refueling his Spirit. That energy was now in control, commanding his body to heal itself and then to serve. His pale skin rippled and undulated as every muscle in his body began writhing to life at once, flexing once again with rediscovered power.

This was not the Lani power of the Reavers, who scavenged life from death, leaving those subjected to their art as either slaves to their new master's will, or as malevolent creatures hungering for the Spirit they no longer fully possessed. Nor did it resemble the healing abilities of some in the Realms who simply enabled natural processes to perform at a faster rate.

No. This was the power of the Goddess Erta Herself, the potency of Creation. The very essence of transforming something that was *not* into something that *was*. Now that same power was coursing through his body, urging him to live so that he could continue his service. His veins were rivers of life. Power coursed through him, each heartbeat sent a current of bliss that washed away all traces of frailty and despair.

As a Seraph, Ge'Lion had always felt the power of Erta in his life, in his body. This time, however, it was different. More urgent. More powerful. More personal. Suddenly infused with Her energy, his green eyes flashed open. Gripping the hilt of the sword that helped reanimate his broken body, he sprang up from his bed and stood tall and proud under the mighty dome where they had laid him to die.

The green-robed attendants were sent scrambling as Ge'Lion brought the Diamond blade of Angios whistling over their heads, then swung it straight up above him in triumph. The sword, reflecting the rays of sunlight streaming in from the high window, blazed like an iridescent

torch, sending the shadows fleeing to the chamber's dark corners. The three Seraph, sprawled upon the white marble floor, watched in silent awe, hope springing to life in their wide eyes. Spellbound, they had witnessed Ge'Lion escape the shadow of death to become once again the embodiment of Erta's glory, in just moments. Standing with a triumphant aura of pride and power under the great dome built in Her honor, he was the seventeen powers made flesh. He was the Realmwalker.

His mind now clear, the dull clouds of his pain-wracked thoughts had been chased away by the wind of Erta's strength within him. Ge'Lion allowed himself a little hope.

It appears I have more time.

But the violent eruptions of pain exploding throughout his body seconds later dwarfed every moment of agony from before. Wave after wave of torment crashed through the old man, shaking the proud shoulders that had once carried the burdens of an entire world. Muscles once bulging with strength were now withered and stretched thin, on the verge of snapping. Knees buckling, he crashed onto the ornately designed stone floor in a quivering, sobbing heap, the great sword falling out from his grip and clattering onto the marble. Darkness leapt at him from the corners to encircle him, the now feeble light of inadequate strength to hold them at bay.

The others, no longer transfixed, scrambled to their feet. Two of them went to the aid of their broken hero, easing him gently back into his bed. The third reverently retrieved the sword, laying it once again at his leader's right side.

Sorry my friend. Apparently not even the Goddess' formidable power can keep this body alive.

Ge'Lion stroked the leather wrapped hilt, as if attempting to soothe the legendary sword.

As the pain continued its inexorable quest of wringing his life away, the nagging question in his mind remained.

Where was the Successor?

The Seraph and history that preceded them taught that there was always a Successor, one ready to take up the Sword when needed. "Erta always provides," was reflexively intoned whenever there was adversity or confusion instead of contentment and understanding. Yet Ge'Lion was on the very brink of death, an inevitability reflected in the faces of the three now watching him with renewed fear and uncertainty. The next Realmwalker, the one to protect the Realms and maintain The Balance had not been found, much less trained, and it weighed heavily on their minds. So much so, that even in his moment of need, only three Naturan Seraph tended to his death bed. All of the other Seraph who could be spared were scouring the Four Realms for any trace of a Successor who was long overdue.

For over three thousand years, the chain had gone unbroken. When death came to a Realmwalker, the Successor was always near, ready to bond with the Sword, prepared to inherit the role of Erta's protector and enforcer. Even when the rogue dragon Firemane ambushed his predecessor, Darba, in Elementa two hundred years before, Ge'Lion was by her side. By that time he had already served five years as Successor and had learned everything he could about the role of the Realmwalker and being a servant of Erta. He had been prepared, ready to take Angios from the fallen heroine's hands, bond with it, and use it to defeat Firemane. Darba was young and in her prime, barely more than twenty years into her service and yet he was there.

Every other passing of a Realmwalker was the same. Either the Seraph found a Successor in their diligent search of the Four Realms, or a Successor arrived at one of the Temples, guided by their Spirit to answer Erta's call. Realmwalkers were unique beings; they were Seraph with the ability to wield all seventeen Lani powers. Regardless of their rarity, they were always found in time. In time to properly train and learn the way of the Realmwalker, anticipating the day effectively foretold from their moment of birth. That day of destiny had come, but the promised Successor was nowhere to be found.

Something is wrong.

Ignoring the pain as he thought about the disruption of history, Ge'Lion began connecting the events leading up to this moment. But a fresh onslaught of suffering was upon him. He had run out of time. Feeling his strength drain away, he still had one important task left to complete.

Moving his hand to touch the hilt at his side, his voice rasped through clenched teeth.

"As bonded we were. Bonded, we shall forever be. Into you, my Spirit I give thee."

He was aware of the servants dropping to their knees, uttering fervent prayers to Erta as the Sword absorbed his Spirit, his life force nearly gone. For the first time in over two hundred years, Ge'Lion's body became an empty vessel.

I am empty.

As he felt the last vestiges of his physical connection to the world fade away, Ge'Lion used his remaining strength to send his own urging to the Goddess.

Call your Realmwalker to you soon, Erta. Help your chosen one protect The Balance. Come to Erta's aid, Realmwalker. Come.

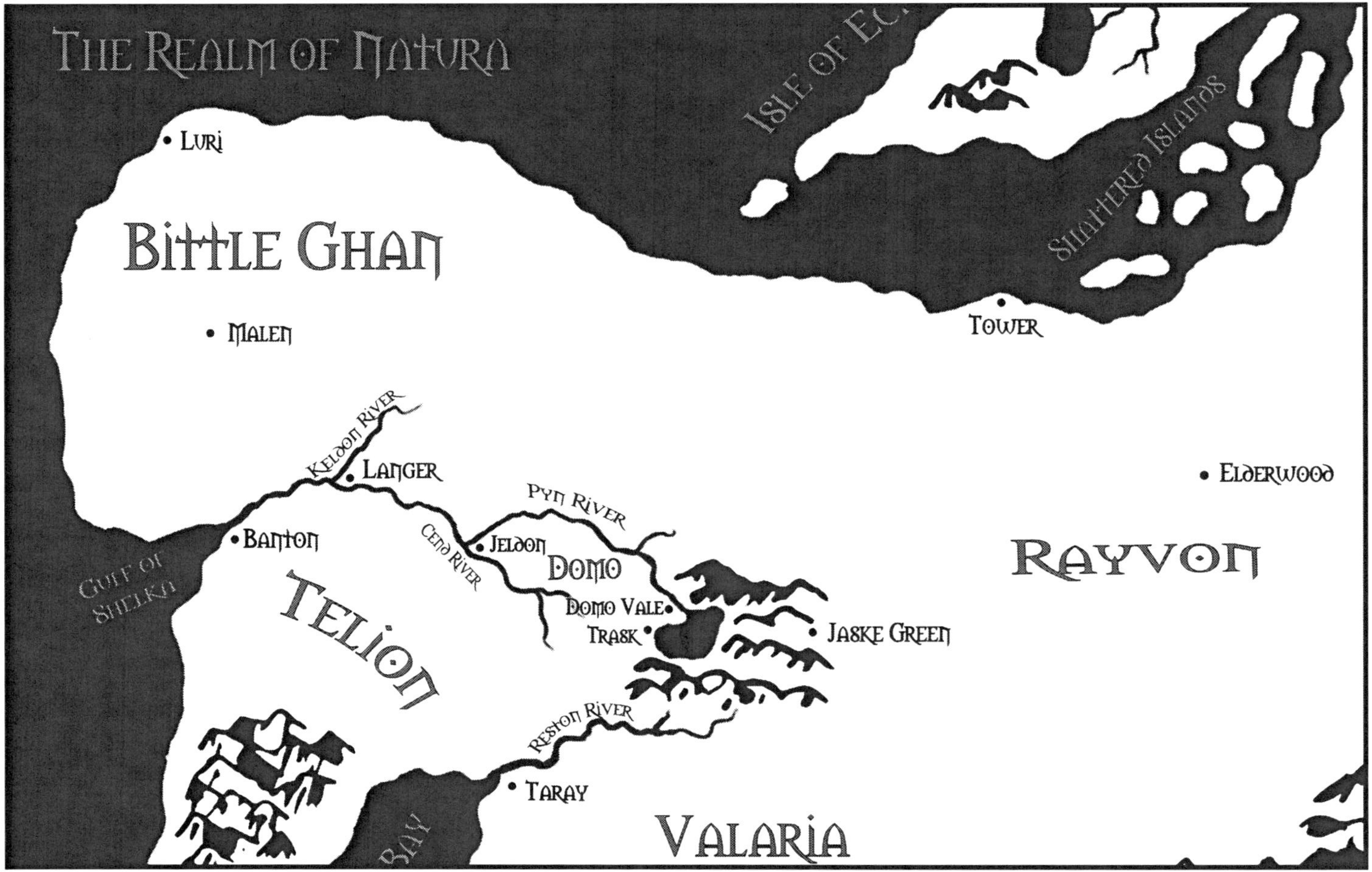

The Realm of Natura
Luri
Bittle Ghan
Malen
Shattered Islands
Tower
Elderwood
Keldon River
Langer
Pyn River
Banton
Cend River
Jeldon
Domo
Gulf of Shelka
Telion
Domo Vale
Trask
Jaske Green
Rayvon
Reston River
Taray
Bay
Valaria

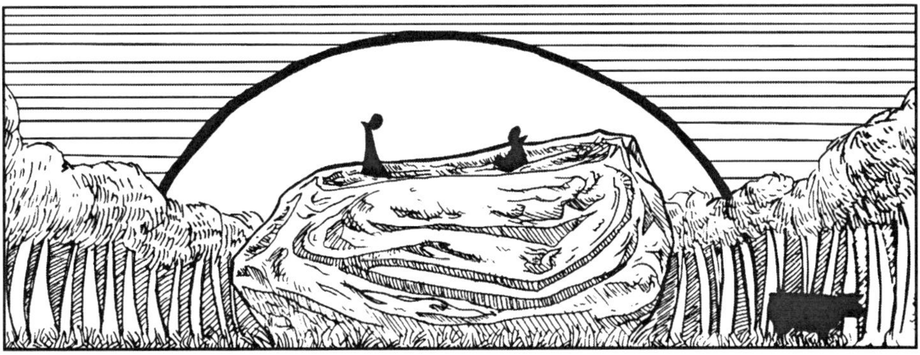

Chapter 1: Upon This Rock

THE forest laid quiet and still, a hint of frost upon the early morning air. With the first light of day still only a glow in the northeastern sky, two shadowy shapes, a smaller one leading one much larger, were moving through a thick stand of trees. They picked their way slowly down a worn, narrow path, meandering through a maze of gnarled tree roots.

The roots appeared to have a mind of their own, threatening to catch both foot and hoof, while the slick, trampled grass and packed earth of the narrow path only made footing that much more treacherous. The smaller shape carefully, but quickly, picked his course amongst the hazards, appearing eager to reach the enclosed grassy meadow ahead.

A dull knock of a hoof upon wood broke the stillness and the animal came to a sudden stop, jerking its head up, almost catching the young man leading it off balance.

"Easy Cassie," Rennick Sherrill said, patting the young cow on her light brown neck. Any one of the roots could have tripped them in the dim light, but it would make matters worse if she continued to panic each time one of her hooves clipped one. Certainly a broken leg—his or the cow's—would make for a bad start to any day. But he was hoping this day be the greatest day of his life, so far. He had walked this path so many times. With or without Cassie, he was sure that he could do it blindfolded. The cow, however, never seemed to get used to it.

"You are just going to have to trust me girl," Rennick said to the somewhat hesitant animal. "Besides, at this meadow you can still get the best of what is left of the first growth grass." The cow, who did not appear convinced, still eyed each potential step on the route through the stand with doubt.

Rennick took up more of the short lead line attached to the cow's halter so he could be closer to her head and better guide her footing. The roots were a nuisance, but not impassable. A few roots now meant that the meadow beyond would be less crowded, better for Cassie's grazing, and for his thinking and daydreaming as well. The maple and willow thicket neatly encircled the entire meadow, also making the clearing an effective enclosure for Cassie so that he could be better about his other pursuits, like sleeping. Today, however, the agenda was thinking.

Well, perhaps a little sleeping.

Rennick was seldom awake at first light to take the family cow out to pasture, but today was a day of special significance, a day of excitement, and perhaps even a day of answers. This was going to be the last day that he had to answer to others, when he was finally able to ask questions and expect answers. He could declare his heart's intentions and others would respect them. Rennick would no longer feel as though he was an untreated wound in Erta's side. He would finally be a purified Neph.

Today, Rennick and his twin sister, Raine, reached their eighteenth year. By finally reaching that age of significance, they would both undergo the Purification Ceremony, cleansing them of their impure heritage, making them new again in the eyes of the Goddess Erta. The twins would then be able to make their Declarations that allowing them to become adults in the eyes of the others in Domo Vale, and throughout the Realm, and to earn their own glyph to prove it. He glanced at the barren space on the inside of each wrist and tried to imagine the Neph glyph, *bandu*, emblazoned upon each one. By becoming both Purified and Declared, a Neph could finally go where his heart desired, begin working the trade he desired, and even marry if he desired.

However, what Rennick desired was for others to finally take him seriously and not to be treated like a child by some and a pariah by others. His mother, Dani, coddled both he and his sister. She worried about them, treating them as if they were made of Chaldan crystal. His father, Jair, was even worse. He insisted that Raine's dream to explore the vastness of Natura was silly and even potentially dangerous thinking. He also refused to teach Rennick what he knew of the ancient fighting style learned by many Neph, The Cou'Rali, though he suspected that his father knew it very well. While the other Neph fathers wanted their boys to join the Realm Guard, or even become one of the lofty Paladins of the Naturan High Guard, Jair seemed to hold no desire for Rennick to be anything other than a common farmer or laborer in Domo Vale.

"There has to be some common folk too," Jair would insist. "A great deal of nobility can be carved out of a good, simple life lived by a good-hearted person." His father always said such things, but they were becoming more frequent and laced with more urgency now that the twins' eighteenth Carna Lunas was upon them.

Carna Lunas, the Festival of Moons, was the seventeen day celebration of The Balance and the gifts of Erta. One day was given to each of the De'Lani to honor Her in its own way and to raise those of age to adulthood. Today was Yelta Luna: The Spirit Moon, the last day of Carna Lunas.

On this day, the most sacred of days for the Seraph of Erta, they held Ceremony in communities throughout the Four Realms. It is then that all of the Neph in the Four Realms celebrating their eighteenth year undergo the process of Purification by the Seraph. Once that is finished and while standing before all those assembled to witness their presentation to adult life, young Neph can Declare their intentions.

It was during their Declarations that two young lovers might announce their engagement or perhaps one would Declare their desire to leave and settle elsewhere. Of course there were many who would Declare their intention to join the Realm Guard or set upon some outlandish quest for personal redemption or glory.

As far as Rennick had heard, the act of Declaration was carried out in much the same manner during Carna Lunas in all Neph and De'Lani communities across the Four Realms. Considered to be the first words uttered as an adult, Declarations carried great weight and meaning, in particular to the one who had spoken them. Within the various Neph communities, however, they were even more revered. A Declaration was honored as the simplest expression of freedom and choice in a life just beginning because the declarer had been denied any freedom or choice until that moment. The Neph embraced it, clung to it, and perhaps even depended upon it.

Rennick led Cassie through the last tangle of maple roots and into the meadow. A few rays of the new day sun pierced the thicket, creating sparks of light that flashed off of frosty blades of grass, while small tendrils of fog clung to the low spots. Fluttering over the treetops, a light breeze carrying the soft, verdant smell of the forest behind him caressed Rennick's short dark hair before losing itself in the grassy sanctuary before him.

Anchoring Cassie's lead line in the ground toward the middle of the meadow, Rennick spied the large flat-topped rock about thirty strides away on the south end of the clearing.

"Maybe I will give you the long line later," he said, patting the cow on the shoulder. Ignoring him, Cassie was already chewing her first mouthful of cool grass as Rennick turned and headed toward the rock. "Have a good breakfast girl," he said.

The flat-topped boulder was about ten feet tall and shaped in a rough circle about twenty feet across. The northern face of the dark granite had a few rough hand holds that he had carved into it a few years earlier, enabling him to reach the top with ease as he scampered up the side.

"I am surprised that you got out of bed this early," said a feminine voice from above as he climbed up.

Startled, Rennick nearly slipped backwards on his final step, but he recovered quickly, managing to bring himself up to the top with only a slight stumble. There, lounging in his favorite spot in the middle of a slight depression on the far side was his sister, Raine.

"There you go again, your mind everywhere else but right in front of you," she said. Light brown, shoulder length hair framed her large, almond shaped eyes as they lightened from light blue to a pale gray. Her eye color, as with all of Maior heritage, displayed both her pleasure and amusement at catching her brother off guard. It was rare when she and Rennick could manage to startle one another. At that moment, it served as true a sign as any of how distracted Rennick's thoughts had become.

For as long as Rennick could remember, he and his sister could always *feel* each other, knowing when the other was near. More recently, if either one focused, they could even point in the direction the other was located. No others but their parents knew of their odd ability, which their father said was likely a result of being twins born minutes apart. Still, they were told to keep it to themselves in case it was considered a manifestation of their mixed heritage and therefore potentially dangerous for them. So it became their own private game, sneaking upon one another without the other noticing. However doing so was becoming nearly impossible to accomplish.

Rennick, feeling his own eyes darkening in embarrassment, was not going to let his sister have such an easy victory over him.

"I believed you to be off to the market or cleaning with Mother. How was I to guess that you would be here, where a male does his work?" Rennick chuckled at the slight darkening in Raine's eyes. He had scored a victory. A small one perhaps, but better than nothing. Raine despised always being expected to help their mother with the traditional feminine chores of Neph societies, while Rennick was always offered the masculine ones by Jair. She considered herself physically superior to any of the young males in Domo Vale and perhaps a large portion of the adults as well.

Standing nearly six-feet tall, Raine was only a couple of inches shorter than Rennick. She was graceful, with an athletic build, and she relished challenging, and more often than not, beating the young Neph males in tests of both skill and endurance. The challenges had been accepted less and less as of late. This was due to the fact that the only person who could beat her anymore was Rennick himself, and even that had become far from routine. He also began to realize not long ago that in the vast number of challenges, the opponents were not as interested in actually winning the challenge as they might have been in winning his sister's attention.

"So, why are you here so early," she said, sitting upright and crossing her long legs before her. "Are you nervous about tonight?"

"I am excited," Rennick replied. "This is the beginning of something for both of us."

Raine looked at him with a knowing lift of her eyebrows, and Rennick relented. "Well, maybe I am a little nervous. Isn't everyone before undergoing Purification and saying their Declarations?"

Raine smiled, her eyes getting lighter, "I suppose. But it is hard for me to be anything but excited."

"You're not even a little scared?" said Rennick. He was excited and ready to move forward with his life, but the actual process frightened him a little, a product of dark dreams from his youth. There were too many things that could go wrong in his opinion, with fatal consequences. Raine herself was one of those things. "Don't you worry something could go wrong during Purification? And what about the Declarations? Have you figured out what you are going to do about them?"

"You are always so worried," she said. "None have died from Purification in years, and you know that I had decided upon my Declarations long ago, regardless of how father will react to them." Raine was smiling, eyes bright, almost white. She truly did seem both excited and at ease, which only made Rennick more unsettled with his own choices. He could feel his eyes darken along with his thoughts.

"But why," he asked. "Why go to serve at the Temple? You know that the Seraph despise us Mixers."

The slur, *Mixer*, was often used by those of pure De'Lani heritage toward the Neph and their parents. According to the Seraph, The Balance was maintained by the four different De'Lani of each Realm living harmoniously together, but choosing their mates only from amongst themselves. This ensured the equal strength and purity of each bloodline's connection to Erta, maintaining The Balance. The Goddess made the separation, according to legend, three thousand years ago to end the cataclysmic Realm Wars, preventing any one De'Lani or Realm in gaining the advantage, strength, or means to overpower the others.

While not strictly prohibited, relationships between individuals of two different De'Lani were strongly discouraged and considered open defiance to Erta's will. For out of these relationships was the possibility of hybrid progeny called Neph. If left unchecked, a Neph would eventually manifest unpredictable hybrid Lani powers that were dangerous, not only to themselves and others, but more importantly, The Balance.

Those who chose to continue their taboo relationship, like Rennick's parents—Dani a Nym and Jair a Maior—were required to accept Spirit branding on their forehead with the bandu glyph and subsequent banishment to one of the Neph societies, small, isolated settlements like Domo Vale. There, forever marked as a traitor to Erta's will, forbidden under the penalty of death from accessing their Lani power, and bound together in forced exile, they scratched out any living possible by farming, hunting, doing menial tasks and physical labor.

But by accepting the consequences, Dani and Jair proved not only their love for each other, but also their loyalty to Erta. Two years after they arrived at Domo Vale, Rennick and Raine were born.

Today it was the twins' turn to honor both Erta's desire and their parent's sacrifices by undergoing Purification. All Neph children were required to participate in the process which permanently removes any latent Lani influences within them, while raising the bandu on their wrists. It was a quick and only slightly painful process, unless of course the Neph had already manifested their Lani power. The experience then became gruesome and drawn out, filled with unimaginable pain and always fatal to the unfortunate youth. It was a horrific, yet necessary part of maintaining The Balance.

Rennick had witnessed the Purification of a manifested Neph only once, but it was a moment that he would never forget.

Dannic Relan, a formidable Maior and Halen Neph, won every footrace and charmed every girl. When he was purified three years before, Dannic's screams tore through their village, lasting for nearly an hour, but echoing in Rennick's nightmares for months.

"After we get the bandu," Raine continued, snapping Rennick out of his dark thoughts, "The Seraph will no longer fear or despise us Ren." Her light eyes were locked onto his. "I feel like I need to do it. I want to see The Pillars and Her Temple with the great domes glittering in the sun. I feel the need to serve the Seraph, help the beings of Natura, and fulfill my part to ensure The Balance." Her eyes brightening even further toward white, Rennick sighed.

It seems like she is certain. Am I?

"I also want to go and explore the world," Rennick said. "To see

Natura, and maybe even find a way to go to one of the other Realms."

Raine snorted as she tried stifling a laugh, "And you think that my ideas are reckless?"

"Well, at least it is on my own terms and not as a lackey," Rennick said. "Plus, it would be a chance to see something that cannot be seen here. You have heard the stories! They say in Elementa, there are De'Lani that can grow wings and fly! And others who can walk on the clouds! Oh, and their Temple is built in the trees of fire! In Mecho they have—"

"Yes, yes, yes," Raine scoffed. "I have heard it all before. You should stop listening to all the 'experts' who gather out in front of the Emerald's Glow. If it is so fantastic, why is everyone not rushing for Beldon or Mank on the next ship to visit?" Her tone was calm, yet it did nothing to hide her contempt. "Oh, I know," she continued. "Because there are no ships that go there. Why? Because we are not supposed to go to the other Realms, that is why. Remember the story of the last person who had the great idea to travel to another Realm?"

Rennick did remember. Last year, a young Maior from Faston Dak Declared that he was going to build his own ship and sail to Elementa. As the story tells it, he and his crew were trying to put out the flames that had engulfed his sails when a huge wall of water slammed into them, extinguishing the flames, but also nearly capsizing his boat. The message was clear, and all he ever saw of Elementa was the glimmer of its distant shoreline. However, Raine was not correct.

"You are wrong," Rennick said. There are ships going to the other Realms all of the time."

Looking out toward Cassie grazing, Raine sighed. "Yes, but only Seraph. They go all of the time, but they never go ashore. Never. They only go to exchange news and update each other on their search for a Realmwalker." Raine looked up at Rennick and shook her head, her eyes darkening as the tone of her voice intensified. "You spend so much of your time worried about me, you never really consider your own decisions. By the Goddess! And you consider me the reckless one?"

Realizing that he had been pacing as they talked, Rennick stopped and stretched out on the cool rock, propping his head up on one arm. At least he could try to look relaxed. He had actually thought a great deal about his Declarations, but he was still torn over what he wanted to do.

He had so much to consider including Raine, his parents, the growing desire to find his place in the world, and a nagging fear of the unknown.

"I did not say that I was actually going to go to the other Realms. But I do feel the same need to leave Domo Vale." Rennick had to be careful with how he approached his next words. Say them wrong and Raine might think that he was only going along to protect her, possibly leading her to Declare that she wanted to leave alone. That would be a disaster. He could not shake the feeling that in some way he was responsible for her safety.

"We could travel together, you and I. Go see great cities like Gran Dak and yes, even the Pillars and the Temple." Rennick hoped she could see he was serious.

"I do not know," Raine said. "Perhaps you should figure out what you really want, find your own life while I find mine."

Rennick knew that one day the time would come for them to live their own lives. But as of now, he did not feel right about leaving his sister alone in the world, especially if she insisted on departing Domo Vale. She needed him, even if she did not admit it to herself. Raine was far too trusting and eager to sacrifice herself to ever make it very far on her own. His true intentions were to see her live a long and happy life, to have her learn the ways of the world, to find someone whom she could love and trust—someone else who would protect her. Until that time, however, it was his job, and he would see it through to its completion, no matter where it would take him.

Besides, the truth was that while their parents were required to stay in Domo Vale, the twins were free to go where they wanted after Ceremony. Rennick did feel the same pull that Raine did, so if she was leaving, he was too. Where she went, he followed. Perhaps he would find the answers he sought in a place beyond what was familiar. He had determined a long time ago that Domo Vale held no answers for him, only more questions. Raine seemed truly set on leaving and was not going to change her mind at the last opportunity.

So that settled it for him. Rennick was going to leave Domo Vale with his sister. If it meant he could help her while also seeing the world outside of Domo Vale, so be it. If she were able to find what fulfilled her without subjecting herself to a lifetime of servitude in the Temple, and he was able to find his answers in the process, even better.

"Raine," he began, his eyes lightening, "I have decided upon my Declarations. I am going to go with you, wherever it is you wish to go, I swear to you this day, upon this rock, that I will see you safely there."

Raine sat looking at her feet in stunned silence. After several moments, she lifted her eyes to meet his, a look of comprehension dawning on her face.

"You were testing me!" she said in a surprised tone. "Why?"

Rennick stood, walked over to his sister, and sat next to her. He looked to the East, past the clearing and over the trees. In the distance, the tree-covered slopes of the Domo Hills rose, marking the eastern boundary of the only world he had ever known. "In case I am somehow chosen to go before you, I had to know that my Declarations were relevant to yours."

He turned to look at Raine, giving her a nudge and flashing a smile. "For all I knew, you had changed your mind and were going to Declare that you wanted to be a barmaid at the Glow."

Raine shot him an exasperated look with darkening eyes. "This is serious, Ren! I cannot have you doing this just to try to change my mind, or worse still, because you have not made up your own."

Rennick kicked a loose stone in frustration, sending it over the side of the boulder. "I cannot explain it, but somehow I know that this is what I am supposed to do." Furrowing his brow, he slowly shook his head. "I won't say that I like what your Declarations are going to be, but I swear that I will help protect you and see you safely to the Temple."

"I understand, and it is nice to know that you care, but I—," Raine's words were interrupted by faint, distant cries for help. She shot to her feet and standing on the flat, gray stone, looked across the field to the north. More cries came from that direction. In a flash Raine, went to the edge and began climbing down the rock before Rennick could get on his feet.

"Come on Ren! Can't you hear that? Somebody needs our help!" she yelled back at him. Catching a glimpse of her eyes, he could see them shining white in excitement.

"Slow down and wait for me," Rennick exclaimed.

His sister launched herself off the side of the rock, dashing off to cross the clearing in the direction of the cries. He climbed down a little more deliberately, but soon he was taking long, swift strides, chasing after Raine who was already halfway across the meadow and passing Cassie. Even with her quick footfalls and flapping cloak, the cow offered nothing more than a casual glance in her direction before reaching down to tear out another mouthful of grass.

"Raine! Will you please slow down and let me catch up?" Rennick flew past Cassie in a dead run, hoping to catch his sister before the trees. With anyone in Domo Vale other than Raine, there would be no doubt in his success. The frost, now turned to dew, had already soaked his heavy-soled boots and he could feel the cool damp on his legs as moisture darkened the lower portion of his leather leggings.

Growing clearer, the call for help rang from the north, growing in urgency and becoming more frantic as they drew closer. Gaining on Raine, he reached the edge of the clearing and the trees just behind her. The cries were coming from the direction of the Pyn River.

Raine slowed only a little as she glanced over her shoulder at Rennick, weaving into the trees and exclaiming, "It's children by the river! Hurry!"

Rennick ran on, also working his way through the trees, now beside Raine, marveling at how smooth and fast she appeared while gliding through them. Adeptly avoiding not only the low branches, but also managing to keep her feet from twisting and fouling on the slick, gnarled roots, Raine flowed. He was able to accomplish much the same, but it felt like he had to expend a great deal more effort than his sister to do so. She had a natural fluidity and efficiency to her movements that he just did not possess.

He began to see openings in the thicket ahead, catching glimpses of the sunlight sparkling off of water and larger patches of blue sky. The ground began sloping down as they approached the river ahead. The cries kept coming, and there was no mistaking them now, the voices were definitely those of children, now only a few strides ahead.

The twins burst out of the thicket and into a still wooded, but more open area surrounding the banks of the Pyn River. One look at the scene in the river before him and Rennick swore. He hated wearing wet clothes.

Chapter 2: To Save a Life

FIVE young Neph were standing on the bank not far from where Raine and Rennick had burst from the thicket. Rennick recognized three of them as part of the Larnich family from Domo Vale. When they spotted the twins running toward them, their cries for help became hopeful pleas and all five of them began shouting and gesturing wildly into the river.

Rennick slowed a little to take in the scene once he had cleared the thickest trees, but his sister never broke her stride, running downstream and looking ahead into the water.

Then he saw the child. A young boy was bobbing with the current of the river which was deep, fast, and dangerous in this particular area. He was clinging to a branch and being carried toward a short section of rapids less than one-half mile down river.

The twins had to act quickly because they would only get one chance at rescuing the child before losing him to the river. There was little hope they would get far enough ahead of the boy before he reached the first short stretch of rapids to attempt to pull him ashore. Isolated as they were, their best opportunity would be to hurry down to the point just past the first section of rapids where a slight bend slowed the current, tending to push objects closer to their side of the river.

Using Cassie's long lead line still attached to his belt was as good a plan as any given their circumstances. Rennick just hoped, by Erta's will, the young boy would make it that far. If they failed to rescue him at that point, he was certain to perish in the next stretch of rapids which was longer and contained several small waterfalls as the Pyn tumbled to the west out of the hills surrounding Domo Vale.

Lungs burning from exertion, Rennick spared some of his breath to yell the plan to his sister. "The bend in the river, he said. "It is our best chance to catch him!"

Raine, now several strides ahead, was angling toward the bank of the river, correcting her course to match the boy's. He was sure she heard him, and thought that perhaps she was staying close to the boy to keep an eye on him. But his apprehension grew, a cold fear paralyzing his heart as Raine sent her cloak, bow, and quiver flying off her body, her own plan obvious. Managing to catch up to the young boy in seconds and turning toward the edge of the bank, which stood six feet above the water's surface, she was gaining speed.

Oh, no!

"Raine! Don't!" It was all that Rennick could manage to say before Raine was launching herself off the bank, diving into the river toward the struggling child.

Tearing the lead line off his belt loop without breaking his stride, Rennick kept his eyes on the two figures, one of them now his sister, in the swirling current. Raine was swimming toward the boy, who was using all of his strength to cling to the branch in the icy, fast-moving water. Each powerful stroke sent her closer to the child, and in a few seconds, she would have him. But that wouldn't matter because by then they would both be tumbling through the rapids.

I have to do something!

The child was counting on Raine, but Rennick knew that she was counting on him. He gritted his teeth.

She is always getting me into trouble!

He ran on, begging his legs to carry him faster. The pulling of air in his lungs felt like he was breathing fire.

Rennick was beginning to realize that leaving them to the fate of even the first set of rapids would likely be fatal to Raine, and certainly fatal to the already tired and nearly drowned boy, who could not have been more than six-years-old. Still at a full sprint, Rennick's eyes met Raine's at the same moment she reached the boy. It was then that Rennick saw his sister grab the branch, and pull herself to the frantic child's side.

Only one chance!

The water was already moving faster and becoming more turbulent as Raine and the boy approached the front of the impending rapids. In seconds they would be in the heart of them.

More time!

Rennick was about twenty strides ahead of the pair and began surveying the situation. Spotting a large rock splitting the river just outside the rapids, a desperate plan began forming. Realizing that he only had one choice, he began shedding his bulky items just as Raine had done moments before.

One chance! More time!

"Hold on Raine! I'm coming," Rennick yelled. Gripping the lead line, he charged the bank, launching himself into the air toward the river.

One chance! More—

Everything around him suddenly took on a slow-moving, surreal quality, and he began to feel everything more deeply. He still felt himself cutting through the air with his body, but the water was no longer moving as swiftly as it had before. Instead it was curling into lazy, frothy ripples and eddies below him.

—time!

The moment disappeared as he hit the cold water, with more force than he had expected, almost knocking the lead line out of his hands, and the air out of his lungs.

Concentrate! One chance!

Rising to the surface, Rennick began swimming across the current toward the large rock, about three hundred feet down river from him and about ninety feet from the bank. Sneaking a glance to where Raine and the child were, he realized that the two were further up river than he thought.

Of course! Raine knew what I would do. She is swimming against the current to slow their approach, giving me more time.

Now within the grasp of the current, any illusion of the Pyn's laziness vanished. He was going to need every inch of the three hundred feet to catch the upriver face of the rock. With each stroke, he alternated between looking at the rock and judging where Raine and the boy were in relation to him. He could see that Raine now had the boy in her right arm, while holding the branch with her left.

As Rennick had hoped, he was still upriver from the massive rock as he pulled himself even with it, allowing the current to carry him toward it. He turned to face the rock and while floating on his back, began to kick against the current, slowing his approach.

Even with his effort, the roiling water slammed him into the rock. Sparks of pain flashing in his eyes, a sharp point he could not see just below the water level tore through the right side of his faded green tunic and ground into his ribs. Fighting back the pain, but still managing to hold the lead line, Rennick shot his right hand under the water. He grabbed the point, while groping the rock face with his left hand for a more secure hold. His hands did not require much, just enough to stop his momentum and stabilize him against the rock. He had to move fast, but haste was his enemy too. Should he slip off the rock's face, or lose the lead line, the residents of Domo Vale would likely be pulling three dead bodies out of the water instead of just one.

Rennick's left hand found a deep cleft about a foot above the surface of the water, allowing him to hold himself against the rock to prepare for his next step. Glancing over his shoulder, he could see Raine was less than fifty feet away, approaching within a few feet to the right of the rock.

Ignoring the protestations of his ribcage, Rennick increased his grip with his left hand and let go of the point with his right, lifting the lead line out of the water. He quickly looped a few inches of the braided leather rope around his hand. He needed a secure hold, but the lead line was only about twenty feet long, and he wanted as much of it as possible to throw toward Raine.

"Raine, get ready," he said. "I am going to throw the line to you!" The roar of the impending rapids was deafening. He saw her nod quickly and he waited for her to draw a little closer.

One chance!

When Raine and the boy were only about fifteen feet away, Rennick threw the coil of line out toward her, whispering Erta's name as it flew through the air. It splashed just inches from the branch she was still holding. Letting go of the branch, she snatched the lead line and twirled it around her hand several times. Rennick could see in her eyes that she was very tired, confirming for him that she had fought the pull of the current to buy him time, all the while keeping both herself and the boy above water without the use of her arms.

Pulling at the line with his right hand, Rennick struggled to maintain a firm grip on the rock with his left hand. Dragging Raine and the boy closer to him and wrapping the slack around his arm gave him more leverage. The more secure hold of the rope allowed him to work faster and pull harder. He could not afford to let them drift downstream of his position, where the drag of the rushing water upon Raine and the boy would tear him off of the rock. With two more quick pulls, he was able to grasp Raine's hand, just as they drew even with him. He pulled them both firmly to the rock, placing her hand on the point that he had used earlier.

The flaw in Rennick's plan was suddenly evident. He could get them to the rock, but eventually he would have to bring them to shore which was still ninety feet away. Tired and cold as they were, he was not certain they had the time to wait for someone to arrive from the village to save them, nor the strength left to fight the current to reach the bank before the rapids. Glancing toward the near shore to see where the other Neph children were, Rennick was shocked to see three strangely tall adults running along the bank with the children following behind.

Nobody could have made it from the village this quickly, but I hope they can help.

He continued to hold the lead line, directing Raine to do so as well, just in case one of them lost their tenuous hold on the slick rock. She smiled at him with a tired, dark eyed expression and looked down at the boy, who was shivering from cold and fear, but otherwise appeared to be unharmed.

For now.

The excitement of the moment made Rennick forget the deep chill of the river, but after seeing the boy, he felt the cold settling even deeper into his body, and he knew they would have to get out of the water soon.

Looking back toward the shore, he saw a thick rope sailing through the air just upriver from them, landing in the water with a splash. The current began carrying the line down toward them.

"Grab the rope!" called a bearded, broad-shouldered man. His deep voice carried easily over the noise of the rapids ahead of them. "We will pull you to shore."

Rennick grabbed the rope when the current carried it into them, and within a few seconds, had managed to secure himself, Raine, and the boy to the end of it. Reaching out of the water, he gave a signal that they were ready before they pushed off from the rock and kicked out into the current.

The rope snapped taut as the river grabbed at them, trying to feed them into mouth of the rapids. They traveled a few feet downstream, but the rope held fast. The combination of Raine and Rennick's kicking, the others pulling them in, and the current itself, angled them toward the water's edge. It was only ninety-feet, but it looked, and felt, like miles.

Finally, their feet struck the river bottom and they were able to stumble and then wade to the narrow strip of mud that lay at the foot of the bank of the river. Exhausted and barely able to move, the twins handed the boy up to waiting hands before gladly accepting help of their own to the top of the bank.

Collapsing onto her back next to Rennick, Raine smiled, her eyes lightening. He was laying on his left side, holding his hand to his ribs where he had smashed it against the rock.

"Took you long enough," she said.

Rennick shook his head. "By the Goddess, Raine, what were you thinking? We could have both been killed!"

Sitting up and running her fingers through her wet and disheveled reddish-brown hair, she dislodged bits of mud, leaves and grass sticking to it. She continued to look at him with that annoying, victorious smile she always wore when she knew that she had done something he would not like, but had to accept.

"I had to test you, Ren. To make sure that you were serious about your intentions, too."

Fuming, Rennick knew that his sister was just making a joke to catch him off guard and hide the fact that, yet again, she put herself in a compromising situation to help someone else. Sitting up gingerly, Rennick lifted his wet tunic to inspect his right side. It was tender and the skin was scraped badly, but no ribs were broken. It hurt and he would likely be sore for a few days, but based on how ripped his tunic was, he felt lucky it was not a great deal worse.

"When are you going to learn that you cannot save everyone," Rennick said. "Sometimes the cost is just too great."

A deep, sonorous voice answered behind him.

"To save a life? No cost is too great."

Rennick, wincing as he stood, turned around to find the tall, broad-shouldered man who had thrown out the rope, leaning against a pine tree. Raine had also risen, and was now standing next to Rennick, bits of leaves and grass still clinging to her hair. The man stood looking at the twins with a mix of confusion and interest, while behind him, one of his companions was setting up wood for a fire.

Raine gasped, then whispered, "His glyph!"

The man, his eyes still studying them, had his left hand on the trunk of the tree while he slowly rubbed the short, but thick, red hair of his beard with the other. In both cases, the glyph on each of his wrists was clearly visible, turning the little warmth remaining in Rennick's body to ice.

A rudimentary image of a being with upraised arms and surrounded by an aura, the glyph was well known and unmistakable. It was the *yelta*, and that only meant one thing. This man was a Seraph.

Chapter 3: Stir of Echoes

WRAPPING himself in a heavy wool blanket and sitting beside a freshly dug fire pit, Rennick sat in amazement as he watched three Seraph go about the process of making a small camp just as he had done many times. He did not know what to expect, but everything appeared to be happening as it should. In fact, he was watching one of the Seraph struggling to ignite the tinder with a flint and steel just across the pit from him. Despite her struggles, there was a grace and dexterity in her movements that he found mesmerizing.

Her.

Shocked, he suddenly realized that this Seraph was female.

Her head shaved, as were all Seraph he had seen, she had on a light leather tunic with matching leggings, both just visible underneath her travel-stained brown cloak. She was quite tall, nearly the same height as Raine, with sturdy shoulders and long legs. All of these things had managed to hide her feminine form from Rennick while he was at first exhausted from the rescue effort, and then distracted by the discovery that their rescuers were Seraph.

After watching her for a few more moments, Rennick realized something else.

She is using flint and steel.

Although it was obvious that she was not experienced in using the small implements, she was still operating them confidently with quick, nimble fingers, putting forth a genuine effort to start a fire. Rennick's mind was having a difficult time accepting what he was seeing. He was witnessing one of the mighty Seraph—a female Seraph—choosing to use the same tools to light a simple campfire that he would have used, and having a difficult time accomplishing the task. He had witnessed several other Seraph over the years ignite the feast fires during Yelta Luna using small sticks that burst into flame when struck together. It was told that they received them as gifts from the Seraph of Elementa, and they would start any fire, even while it was raining. What he was witnessing now was like watching a bird climb a tree.

He considered offering her assistance, but as soon as the thought occurred to him, he was already dismissing the idea. She had a determined look that told Rennick that they would freeze to death before she would have ever given up trying let alone accept help from anyone, much less a Neph.

After a couple of minutes, a thin line of pine-scented smoke began rising up slowly from the small pile of bark, needles, and twigs she hovered over. Pursing her full lips, she gently blew on the smoldering heap, causing a small tongue of flame to appear, bringing a wide smile of satisfaction her face. Her smile faded slightly as she glanced up. Her two large, deep brown eyes locked on to Rennick's suddenly darkening eyes. Unable to look away, a strange combination of fear and longing began seeping into him through that gaze.

By Erta, is she beautiful!

As she crouched over the growing fire, thin tendrils of smoke began winding around her, caressing her face, accentuating the curves of her body he could not believe that he missed before. His observing became staring, with her eyes holding him as firmly as if she were gripping his hands.

Rennick's heart was pounding and he could feel his eyes grow darker while a warm blush began flooding his cheeks. He was embarrassed for watching her struggle when she sent him a broad, flashing smile, sending his heart racing faster.

“My first fire,” she said in a soft, even voice, her deep brown eyes glittering with the growing flames. Then giving him a quick wink, she stood up, turning to the small pile of dead branches laying nearby and began adding several to the fire. After adding the wood, she assembled a cooking tripod over the fire.

Rennick was thunderstruck.

She winked at me!

A barely stifled laugh at his side shattered his trance. He turned to look at his sister sitting beside him. Wearing a taunting smile, she seemed on the verge of raucous laughter.

“New girlfriend?” she whispered, the lightening of her eyes mocking the continued deepening of his own.

“No, I think she was just trying to embarrass me since I saw her have so much trouble with that fire.”

“That smile was not meant to embarrass you,” she said. “Trust me. A girl only smiles like that for one reason.”

“Raine!” Rennick hissed. He was sure the Seraph could hear them.

“I am just saying that—,” she began to reply, but he interrupted.

“She is a Seraph! Seraph! Or have you forgotten?” Rennick’s tone was now a harsh whisper. “We are Neph!”

Knowing that his eyes must have been nearly black at that point, Rennick felt as if he were speaking loud enough for the entire camp to hear him. He knew that Raine was just teasing, but he guessed that none of the Seraph, the female in particular, would find it very amusing if they overheard their topic of conversation.

“I am quite sure that these three are the same that were supposed to arrive in Domo Vale for Ceremony today,” he said, softening his voice. His sister’s eyes darkened a little more with each word, as she turned toward the fire and studied the flames. Like him, she was probably beginning to wonder if the Seraph would have bothered to save any of them had they known they were rescuing three impure Neph.

Turning his attention back to the others in the camp, Rennick was thankful that Raine let the conversation end. The male Seraph who had spoken to the twins earlier was hanging a small brass kettle filled with water on the tripod. After adding a small handful of crushed leaves and stirring the mixture with a wooden spoon, he stood and looked at the female Seraph still kneeling by the fire, holding her hands out to its growing warmth.

"Nicely done Jirri," he said to her in a pleased tone. "Do not be concerned with how long it took to accomplish the task, be only concerned with how you succeeded."

"Thank you, Kanias," she replied, nodding her head slowly, "I will remember to do so."

"Now please, have these youths lead you back to their village so you can inform their families as to what occurred and that all is well," Kanias said, gesturing toward the five young Neph standing huddled nearby. "After Tarien and I finish with the camp and our other three guests have recovered sufficiently from their ordeal, we will return them to the village." His eyes passed over the three of them as they huddled closer to the heat from the fire. He added, "It should not be long, as they appear to be quite resilient."

Jirri stood and walked over to Tarien, a thin, finely muscled male Seraph with sharp, angular features and a faint olive tint to his skin. He was standing with the five young Neph who were accepting what appeared to be small, hard biscuits he was offering them.

As they stood looking at the round biscuits with nervous curiosity, Jirri took a one out of Tarien's hand and took a bite, her infectious smile once again gracing her lips. The youngest of the group, one of the Larnich brood, followed her lead and nibbled one side of the treat. A sudden smile split his face as he popped the rest in his mouth and began chewing eagerly.

"May I have another," he managed to ask in spite of the mouthful, prompting the other four to look at each other and simultaneously bite into their own biscuits. Jirri watched as smiles blossomed on all of the faces around her.

"It is called *maoli*," Jirri said, before taking another small bite of her own. "Maior sweet bread. Typically, maoli is travel food, but every time that I eat one, I remember my grandmother making them for me when I was young. I will tell you the story as you take me to your village." The children encircled Jirri, appearing excited about not only hearing a story from a Seraph, but also leaving the river behind. Glancing over, she nodded at Tarien.

The wiry Seraph reached into the small burlap bag he was carrying and handed each child a second maoli, this time accepted by eager hands. As they began nibbling their treat, Jirri led them out of the camp, heading in the general direction of Domo Vale. Disappearing into the trees, Rennick heard a chorus of young voices as Jirri asked for directions to the village.

Their voices slowly fading away into the forest to the southwest, Tarien watched them leave for a little while and then turned to put away the bag of maoli, either forgetting or choosing not to offer the other three any of the sweet bread. Rennick frowned. Because of the children's reactions, he had been looking forward to tasting one of Jirri's treats. Although the twins were half Maior on their father's side, Rennick had never heard of maoli before. It did not surprise him, however. Joining the Neph typically meant leaving everything behind, even family traditions, behind.

"Please do not take offense," Kanias said, noticing Rennick's frown. "I believe that Jirri's love for her grandmother's memory has already left us with barely enough for the three of us on our return to the Temple. We will likely have to purchase additional provisions before we leave your village."

Rennick turned toward the Seraph, who was kneeling by the fire. Kanias took the lid off the brass kettle, once again stirring the boiling liquid with the spoon. A sharp aroma filled the air, hinting of mint and spice; it made him warmer just smelling it. Out of the corner of his eye, Rennick saw Raine straighten up and look to the burly Seraph.

"Master Seraph, were you and your companions traveling to Domo Vale?" she asked.

"Please, please!" he said. "Call me Kanias. We were dispatched to your village for Yelta Luna and Ceremony," he continued, while pouring the steaming tea into tin cups. "May I have your names?" He gave a cup to each of them, beginning with Raine.

"My name is Raine Sherrill, and this is my twin brother, Rennick," she said respectfully. "We are to be participating in the Ceremony tonight." Raine said in a matter of fact tone before she stopped to sip her tea.

Rennick accepted a tin cup from Kanias' hands, but did not immediately drink it, choosing instead to inhale the pungent steam rising from the liquid with suspicion. He tried to look as if he were blowing to cool the tea, but when he looked up, his eyes met the Seraph's, who was watching him with amusement. Kanias handed the last cup he held to the young boy, who was in the process of saying that his name was Garen Larnich.

"I am not going to go through all the trouble to save you three from the river, only to poison you, Rennick," Kanias said. "Besides, I have some questions for the two of you, Raine and Rennick Sherrill."

"Questions? For us?" Raine sounded as confused as Rennick felt.

"Well," Kanias said, wearing a thoughtful expression, "I was wondering if there was anyone else with you, or if either of you saw anyone else nearby when you came to save young Garen?" Kanias' rugged features took on the same mixture of confusion and interest that Rennick had seen on his face before.

Raine shook her head slowly, glancing first at Kanias, then at Rennick. "My brother and I were alone, and I did not see anyone until we came to the river and found the children. Did you see anyone, Ren?"

Finally sipping his tea, Rennick shook his head. While the heat of the fire and the invigorating scent of the tea had coaxed some of the warmth and flexibility back into his limbs, that little sip was sent waves of heat through him, finishing the job.

Kanias stood, looking at both of them with an unreadable expression on his face. "Please, it is critical that you tell me the truth. I mean you no harm, I swear by Erta."

Raine looked up at Kanias while taking another sip of her tea. "I assure you, Kanias, we would not lie or mislead you."

For a few seconds Kanias studied them, then nodded. "I apologize for suggesting that either of you would do so. The woods are fairly thick, even close to the river. It is possible for you to have not seen someone, even nearby."

Raine flashed a glance in Rennick's direction. "Excuse my curiosity, but why do you believe that someone else was nearby?"

Rennick was suddenly uneasy. He could tell by the change in the look on Kanias' face that he was debating with himself. The burly Seraph looked over at Tarien, who had rejoined them beside the fire, kneeling next to it while rubbing his hands over the flames. As the Seraph looked over to meet Kanias' gaze, Rennick thought that he saw the slightest shake of the wiry Seraph's head. Returning his gaze to the fire, Kanias was silent for a couple of seconds before closing his eyes and sighing.

"As we approached the river to investigate the children's cries for help, the three of us all felt a unique Lani power being used. It lasted but a few seconds, disappearing just as we broke through the trees and finding you three in the river."

Opening his eyes, Kanias stood, reaching for the kettle and another cup, then pouring himself some of the remaining tea. After returning the kettle, he turned away from the fire and walked a couple of paces toward the Pyn. Bringing the metal cup to his lips, he looked out at the river, sparkling in the late morning sun. "I was hoping to find someone other than a few young Neph," he said before taking another sip from the cup.

An awkward silence blanketed the camp, interrupted only by the occasional popping and hissing noises from the flames. Tarien, still crouching by the fire, was studiously ignoring the three Neph, but looked like a tightly wound spring. The boy, Garen, who sat near the thin Seraph, appeared ignorant of the sudden tension as he idly picked at a frayed corner of his blanket. Rennick flicked his eyes up to Kanias as the Seraph continued watching the river, sipping his tea. Rennick thought that Kanias appeared sad, perhaps even disappointed. Suddenly, a thought occurred to Rennick:

He believes that one of us has manifested early!

He turned his head, glancing toward his sister. Raine had fallen silent again, and she did not meet is eyes, choosing instead to stare intently into the fire. Her deep blue eyes were glimmering from the barely held tears welling within them. A deep chill, earlier chased away by the fire and wonderful tea, returned far colder and harsher than before, speeding up Rennick's spine and washing over him, turning his whole world to ice.

Raine!

The echoes of the past were suddenly stirring again in Rennick's mind, breathing cold life into unwelcome thoughts. They were the remembered screams and horrific sounds of a dying youth. Unlike his memories and dreams of Dannic Relan, however, the screams that thundered through Rennick's mind now were those of his sister.

Chapter 4: A Fear and a Dread

HIS head spinning, Rennick's thoughts were a swirl of torment and despair amid the deafening silence that continued to smother any bit of conversation that erupted around the fire. The only sound that Rennick could hear was his pounding heartbeat in his ears. The camp's din was muted, but the tension became palpable, taking on a life of its own in the smoky air.

The silence was finally broken by Kanias as he turned away from the river to address Tarien. "I believe that we should purchase our provisions today, Tarien, before Ceremony. I want to make sure that we are fully stocked and prepared for travel before the village becomes too occupied with today's activities."

Nodding his approval, Tarien rose from his spot by the fire and walked to a small clearing a few strides away. There, three horses, each tied to a tree, casually searched the ground around their hooves for the sparse grass that grew in the shade. At the foot of each horse's tree sat several piles of saddles, blankets, saddlebags and other gear. Kneeling next to one of these piles, Tarien began sorting the contents, making a meticulous evaluation of each item.

Kanias stood watching Tarien for a moment before turning back to stare out over the river and resume sipping his tea.

Occupied with today's activities? More likely, he means 'Upset and possibly angry when Raine dies from Purification.'

While Yelta Luna always held a very festive and celebratory atmosphere, Rennick knew it to be a mere facade for the undercurrent of fear that ran through the families and friends of loved ones preparing for Purification. Parents of a Neph participating in the rite, in particular, were very sensitive during this time, for they knew that it was only through their past decisions that this day was required.

Leading up to a Neph's eighteenth Yelta Luna, his or her parents would keep a close watch, looking for any sign of early manifestation of Lani abilities. It did not change what was to occur, and it did not help the youth survive the inevitable outcome, but it gave the family the ability to choose a less gruesome fate for the unfortunate child.

Rennick had heard stories of parents slipping pollen from a Nightwhisper blossom into their newly manifested child's food or drink, making them fall into a peaceful sleep from which they would never awaken. There were also parents who made arrangements for the child to leave or escape into the wild on their own, leaving their fate for Erta to decide.

Such interventions, however, were considered by the Seraph to be a deliberate upsetting of The Balance and a defiance of Erta's will, and were greatly frowned upon. The Seraph believed and taught that the process of Purification was a form of Erta's judgment which was for Her alone to make.

In the case of those who decided to run away, they were tracked down. If found alive, they were brought back to the village. Then the child and all those who assisted in the escape were submitted to Erta's judgment through Purification. The Balance demanded assurance that the hybrid was removed, and any effort to circumvent Erta's judgment would not be tolerated.

Thinking it all through as he stared into the fire, Rennick realized that he was trying to discover a way to get Raine out of her predicament, but history told him that his efforts would be fruitless. When families Domo Vale faced this situation, they learned very quickly to say goodbye. Rennick would either have to accept Raine's fate or find a way to defy it.

The echoing of voices and the snapping of twigs underfoot came from the trees to the southwest of the camp. They startled Rennick from his thoughts, reminding him of where he was in an instant. Looking in that direction, he saw Jirri picking her way through the brush to reach the clearing that held their campsite. Just behind Jirri, walked Jair, the twins' father. Jair's powerful voice was clipped, but as it forced its way through the trees, it filled the camp's already anxious air with anger, making Rennick cringe.

"—should have enough sense not to be jumping into the Pyn and troubling Seraph with their recklessness." Jair's tone was furious in the distance. Rennick heard his sister sigh behind him as he noticed Tarien rise slowly from his work on one of the bundles of gear and lean against a nearby tree where three metal-clad quarterstaves stood. No doubt, Tarien was expecting trouble.

This could get bad. I need to calm father.

"I assure you, Master Sherrill, that your children were only doing what they thought was right," Jirri replied over her shoulder in a soothing voice. "They were quite brave, and certainly saved that boy's life."

"Well, that remains to be seen, Seraph, but knowing my children, they were more concerned about being heroes than determining if there were safer ways to accomplish the task," Jair said as he strode past Jirri to the edge of the camp.

Scanning those around the fire, Jair first spotted Raine rubbing the tears out of her eyes, and then locked his dark eyes onto Rennick. He started down the small slope and began rounding the fire toward Rennick, his face red with fury.

"You both have some—" his father began.

"Master Sherrill, is it?" Snapping to attention, Kanias quickly interrupted, turning from the river bank. "I am Seraph Kanias Ondrell, and we are honored to welcome the father of these two heroic youths into our camp," he said while stepping around Rennick, intercepting Jair.

To Rennick's shock, Kanias smiled and then bowed to his father. As he bent at the waist, Kanias bent his arms at the elbows, bringing his hands to waist level, palms facing up and crossed right over left, the glyph on each wrist clearly visible. He brought his head to his fingertips and then rose again, putting his hands at his sides. It was a bow normally reserved for greeting an equal in a formal setting.

"Y—yes, Lord Kanias." Jair said, fumbling his words, obviously as stunned as Rennick was and returning the gesture. Jair appeared hesitant to touch the bandu on his forehead with his fingertips. "I am Jair Sherrill, and I hope you can forgive me for my desire to weigh their bravery myself," he continued in a steadier voice after rising from his bow.

"It is true, Master Sherrill," Kanias began as he wandered over to where Garen sat by fire and cupped the young boy's face in his hands as if studying him. "Garen here would have perished had it not been for their decisive action." His tone was direct, but his courteous smile and relaxed posture was in sharp contrast to Jair's fierce countenance.

"Seraph Jirri already gave me a brief account of the rescue, Master Kanias. My question to my children is what would they have done had you three not been near at hand to assist them?" Jair was respectful in his reply, but he made clear a sense of doubt regarding the Seraph's appraisal of the twins' role in the rescue.

Rennick could see out of the corner of his eye that Tarien was now holding one of the three quarterstaves, cradled in his arms, looking as if he had been holding it the entire time. It was obvious to him that Tarien believed he might have to subdue Jair. With everything that had already happened that morning, the last thing the residents of Domo Vale needed was a physical incident with the Seraph on Yelta Luna.

Possessing of a tall, long limbed frame, powerful from years of hard farm labor and a presence of complete physical confidence, Jair was intimidating. But these were Seraph. Mighty. Authoritative. Wielders of the four Lani powers. Moreover, it was a death sentence to strike one of Erta's Chosen. If not by law, then by consequence.

"Father—," started Raine.

A single glance from Jair silenced Raine, his deep blue eyes blazing. Rennick saw her eyes darken before she looked away, staring again into the fire.

"We were only trying to help," Rennick said in a rush. Jair spun to face Rennick, eyes afire with dark light. It took all that he had not to recoil from his father's gaze.

"You!" Jair's body was tense with fury. "You are already treading on dangerous ground with me, after the disappearing act you pulled this morning. I told you to stay close to home today." His face softened and eyes lightened a little as he stole a glance to take in the three Seraph.

Rennick's resolve broke down. He knew that his father's concern was that the young Neph would run away, or even appear to run away during Carna Lunas. Not only were such things topics of shame and scandal among the Neph, but retribution was often sought by some in the community who feared that any disobedience could be seen as seeds of rebellion, leading to sanctions and wider prejudice against them. Some Neph even worried about their kind being outlawed and exterminated all together.

"It is time that I take you two back home and end our burden on the Seraph. They have much to attend to before Ceremony." Jair said, softening his demeanor even more. "Besides, we have already taken too much of their time."

Tarien did not move. Something changed in the air around the wiry Seraph that made him appear to relax. Rennick exhaled a deep breath he did not realize he had been holding.

"By your leave, Master Sherrill, I would like to accompany you as I return Garen to the village," Kanias said, his manner assuming Jair's agreement. "I will require directions to where the Larnich household is located."

Jair stood staring briefly at the Seraph, a shadow of concern passing over his face, then nodded his head. "As you wish, Seraph Kanias," he said. The Larnich home is on the other side of the village from ours, but I will show you the way. First, we will need to recover the twins' things upriver, and our cow, which if I am not mistaken, will be in a clearing just to the south. Then, we will stop by our home along the way so the twins can rest after their ordeal."

Kanias nodded in assent. Turning toward Jirri he beckoned with a thick hand for Tarien to join them. He proceeded to give her some instructions regarding various small chores still to be completed at the camp before walking with Tarien over to the horses. There, Kanias began taking a few items out of one of the saddlebags beside one of the horses. He did not look up as he searched deeper into the leather bag, but he spoke in an inaudible murmur to Tarien. The younger Seraph did not appear very pleased, but said nothing, before nodding slowly, turning on his heel, and heading south out of the camp.

With the three Seraph's attention elsewhere, Jair turned to whisper Rennick and Raine. "Not one word about this morning until we are alone at the farm."

Walking back to the fireside, Kanias approached Garen, lifting him up and placing him upon his thickly muscled shoulders, much to the delight of the young Neph. "Lead the way, Master Sherrill," he said. I have taken the liberty of sending Tarien to recover your cow. He will let the animal lead him back to your farm. If you do not mind, I would love to chat with you regarding your village. It is said that you are someone of considerable influence among those who live in Domo Vale."

"I do not know about influence, Master Seraph, but I will answer any questions you may ask to the best of my ability," Jair replied.

It appeared to Rennick that his father had relaxed considerably over the past few minutes, telling Rennick that perhaps his father was only reacting to his initial shock of the events, and upon seeing that the situation was okay, was calming down. Raine still refused to meet their eyes, and he could see that she was still confused and worried. Rennick was certain that she was feeling the inevitability of what was to come at Ceremony, as it weighed on his mind also.

He glanced at his wrists, where a bandu glyph would appear on any Purified Neph. For as long as he could remember, he had wanted that mark, a sign of both his bondage and freedom. He had dreamed of receiving his glyphs, knowing that they meant open doors for both himself and his sister. Now all of that was in jeopardy. He was feeling as trapped as Raine looked.

As they made their way upriver out of the campsite, Rennick had a sudden compulsion to look back, and he was surprised to meet eyes with Jirri, who was kneeling near a small pile of gear by the horses. His pace slowed as a feeling of being measured and surveyed by those deep brown eyes overcame him, sending a mix of exhilaration and invasion rippling through him. She was Delving him. Just as he was about to break eye contact, Jirri averted her eyes and went back to digging into a leather satchel.

"Is everything alright, Rennick?" said Kanias, who appeared next to him just as Rennick began to turn away from Jirri and the camp. Raine and Jair continued to walk, and were a handful of strides ahead. They stopped and turned slowly to look back at Rennick and Kanias. Rennick began to walk towards them, but the Seraph locked his bright green eyes on him. He felt his own eyes darken under the weight of Kanias' piercing stare.

"Yes, everything is fine," Rennick replied. He felt embarrassed and was concerned that Kanias might have thought that he was flirting with Jirri, and was more than happy to dismiss the situation. The troubled look passing over Kanias' face, however, made it clear that the Seraph did not like Rennick's answer. The uncomfortable feeling of being measured overcame him again, but this time the feeling was emanating from Kanias. Rennick's apprehension grew at being Delved twice by two different Seraph in a span of several moments, but it lessened as he witnessed the melting of concern off of Kanias' face. The Seraph's face then grew with a look of amazement before finally blossoming into a wide smile.

"Yes, everything is just fine, young Rennick. Fine indeed," Kanias said with a hearty chuckle. "Come along now. I am sure that you are eager to get home." Turning, Kanias then gazed upon Raine, still standing next to Jair several strides away. A slight widening of her dark, downcast eyes and the rise of color on her cheeks told Rennick that he was Delving her now. Kanias' smile growing even larger, he said softly, "Yes, you are both very well indeed."

"What is going on?" demanded Jair. "What are you doing to the children, Master Kanias?"

"In all of the chaos, with the rescue, taking care of the other children, and your arrival, I had not taken the time to properly Delve your children to ensure that they were not harmed in any way by the incident. I just did so, and aside from Rennick's bruised ribs and some exhaustion, all is well. In fact, I am quite surprised with what I discovered." Kanias, still smiling and carrying Garen on his shoulders, moved to rejoin Raine and Jair, with Rennick walking after him.

"What did you discover," requested Jair with a sight narrowing of his darkening eyes. Kanias walked up alongside Jair and Raine and leaned in toward them.

"Not here. Not now, Master Jair," Kanias' eyes rolling up to take in

Garen. "These are matters best discussed with only the family present."

Jair's eyes, darkening still further, told Rennick that his father was not pleased with being denied an explanation by Kanias, but the hint of resignation in his manner also told him that he also agreed with the Seraph. Kanias continued smiling, as the five of them continued upriver through the trees. An even darker cloud of silence descended over Jair.

It was not long before they came across Rennick's quiver and bow laying on the ground, and his cloak partially draped over a short, squat bush. It seemed that it was days ago when he had discarded those items, and launched himself into the river.

After collecting his belongings and fastening them firmly to himself, the others followed Rennick as he led them to where Raine's items lay. They appeared further upriver than he had remembered, but they were still in good order and it was not long before Raine had them affixed to her. The five of them, led now by Jair, turned southwest to cut through the trees to meet the portage trail.

After a short while, they came upon the portage—a wide, well-worn path that had been made by the residents of Domo Vale. Taking the path to the southeast would lead them back toward Rennick's clearing, as well as some of the small Maior dominated settlements that dotted the foothills around Domo Lake.

The path had been worn smooth by the years of foot, hoof and wagon traffic between the village and the shores of the lake. The villagers traveled often to the lake to cast nets in the clear waters for the plentiful fish, and traders used it as a portage to avoid the rapids between the lake and Domo Vale.

The village, sitting two miles to the northwest, was nestled against the south bank of the Pyn River just below the same rapids that Raine and he had just fought so hard to avoid. At that point, the widening river flows more slowly, making it an ideal staging area for the river boats moving dried fish, meat, lumber, and other goods to the many towns and settlements located along the Pyn. Some of the boats made it all the way to the port city of Banton, where the Pyn empties into the Gulf of Shelka. From there, the relatively small amount of goods from their village joined those from all over the region in the massive trade ships bound for the vast markets found in the cities in Dakeon and Beldon. It was rumored that some items even made it onto Seraph ships bound for the other Realms, but Rennick always believed it to be wishful thinking.

As they arrived at the wider path, Kanias began asking Jair some questions regarding Domo Vale, which were answered with curt answers or grunts of affirmation. Jair's bad mood had returned, or perhaps he simply had given up any pretense in trying to hide it. The Seraph inquired about the quality of the first growth harvest, the amount of trade traffic heading downriver, and the relations of the Neph with the surrounding communities. However, with each question, it appeared that Jair was growing more impatient, and began increasing his pace, forcing the others to walk faster.

After a while, just as the land began sloping away toward the river, and the taller buildings of Domo Vale became visible above the tree tops ahead, they came upon the narrow lane cutting into the mix of fir and oak trees south of the main path which led to the Sherrill's small farm. Tucked into a secluded clearing, Rennick could see glimpses of their low, flat-topped home and the high-peaked roof of the barn through the trees that lined the lane.

"Master Seraph," Jair said in an assuming manner, "If you would excuse me for a moment, I am going to walk with my children to the house. I also think that it would be best if I let my wife know all is well, as she surely has heard about the excitement at the river by now." Without appearing to protest, or taking offense, Kanias lifted Garen off of his shoulders and indicated that the young Neph should sit in the grass to one side of the lane.

"Of course. If all is well, I will return later," Kanias replied as he watched Garen sit and pick at the grass. "There is a matter that I would like to discuss with your family regarding Ceremony."

Rennick's blood froze with the casual nature in which Kanias spoke. He did not need to see Jair stiffen, or Raine fidgeting to know that they were startled by it as well.

By the Goddess, he is talking about Raine!

Glancing at Raine, he was surprised to meet her gaze but less so to see the shadow of fear over them. Attempting to be reassuring and strong, he flashed an awkward smile toward her. Instead of reassuring and strong, however, Rennick was sure he appeared conflicted and weak.

Kanias turned toward Raine and Rennick and formally bowed to each of them. "Until we meet again, young Raine and Rennick Sherrill. I am truly honored that the Goddess brought us together on Her day."

Springing up, Garen ran up to Raine and hugged her legs. "Thank you, Raine, for helping me. You are amazing." Then he turned, smiled at Rennick, and ran back to Kanias who patted him on the back with approval. The Seraph wore a huge smile on his face as he looked back up at the twins. Raine had a sparkle and slight lightening of her eyes, masking the concern and worry residing there only moments before.

Jair grunted and turned down the lane, motioning to Raine and Rennick to follow. "Just a couple of minutes, Master Seraph, and I will return," he called over his shoulder.

"Take your time, Jair," Kanias replied, "We will wait here for you."

Walking down the lane, Raine and Rennick bracketed their father on either side. Curious, Rennick glanced over his shoulder. He could see Garen and Kanias sitting in the grass at the end of the lane, the boy peppering the Seraph with questions. They went unanswered, as Kanias sat silently, watching the three of them walk away, a broad, satisfied smile on his lips. Rennick looked away quickly, his mind filling with worry and concern.

I need to speak alone with Father! He needs to know about Raine before he goes back to the Seraph, who seems far too pleased at the prospect of Purifying a manifested Neph.

Looking over at Jair as they strode up the lane, Rennick could see that his father's face was a mask of steely determination, his dark eyes reflecting dark thoughts, shattering the illusion of the calm display earlier. It made what Rennick had to say even more difficult, but he caught a glimpse of his sister walking on the other side of their father, and her face convinced him it was time to act. Caught somewhere between happiness and fear, elation and desperation, Raine was locked in a struggle of competing emotions, struggling to take it all in, like sunlight in a tornado of shadow.

As they approached their home, Rennick took in the surroundings to help calm his inner turmoil. This was home. It was here where he and Raine were safest. The low pitch, one story house had a sod roof thick with deep green grass. It was speckled with small white flowers that filled the air with a light scent that meant home to him. Modest, but comfortable. His mother, Dani, had seen to that. On one corner of the roof, a short ladder provided access to the small garden Dani planted every year since the twins had been born. As a Nym, she believed that plants played a crucial role in The Balance, and that included how they fit into the role of nutrition. So they grew various herbs and vegetables to supplement their diet of milk, cheese, fish and the occasional field hen. The well-tended front yard was clipped short by Cassie's daily grazing.

Finally arriving at the house, Jair's silence ceased. His voice was low and punctuated with urgency. "Where is your mother?"

Chapter 5: Decisions

FOLLOWING Jair through the heavy hide and oak door, Rennick walked into their home with Raine close behind. It was obvious that his father was not pleased to find their mother not inside, and repeated with exasperation, "Where's your mother?"

"She said that she had items to pick up for Ceremony tonight at the village," Raine offered. "She needed some beads to finish my dress, and some dye for Ren's new tunic, among other things."

"We do not have much time," Jair replied as he turned to face them. Mixed emotions coursed over his ruggedly handsome face. Fear. Doubt. Anger. Hope.

I have to tell him now.

"Father, we have a problem." Rennick said slowly, and he saw Raine look toward him out of the corner of his eye. "The Seraph Kanias believes that Raine has manifested early."

"Wait!" Raine exclaimed. "It is not me who has manifested early Rennick. You have!"

Jair, stunned to silence, looked first at Rennick, and then at Raine, his eyes darkening. Raine's eyes were rimmed again with tears. She turned her eyes down to look at her feet, shuffling them in a nervous dance.

"What is happening, Raine?" Jair demanded, "Please tell me everything, quickly."

"When I was in the river, I saw Rennick move like a D'ware," she started slowly, but her voice grew stronger when she looked up at their father's eyes. "He ran so fast, he was a blur, and when he jumped into the river, it was like he was shot out of a bow."

Rennick was numb to the point of speechlessness. Yet even in the fog, he knew that there was something wrong about what she was saying. "But Raine, I am not D—" he trailed off as a word came up in his mind like the bile in his throat.

Mixer.

Of all the words, that one was used to denote the dangers of Neph. Unpredictable hybrid abilities. He remembered the lazy way the river moved below him, and the force at which he hit the water, and he realized the truth.

I have manifested.

Rennick's world swayed. Jair's rough, strong hand caught Rennick's shoulder as he fought to regain his equilibrium. "Easy, son," said Jair in a strangely soft and smooth voice. "We will take care of this. Raine, please tell me everything that happened and was said before I arrived at the camp."

Taking slow, deep breaths, Rennick listened as Raine recounted all of the events that happened from the river rescue to Kanias explaining that they had felt the ability used, which led them to the river. "I thought it was you, Raine," said Rennick. Looking up, he saw Raine's eyes filled with the tears of sympathy and fear for him.

Jair sprang to action. "We are leaving Domo Vale."

***

"Master Seraph, I'm hungry," the young Neph Garen said for the third time in as many minutes.

Kanias sighed, giving a soothing gesture to the child as his eyes never left the farm. He was troubled. Garen needed to get home soon as their trouble at the river had surely been reported by now, and he could not keep the young child away for much longer before panic started to ripple through the village.

All of the Neph settlements were the same. While the villages were always very accommodating to visiting Seraph, treating them with great honor and reverence, he could always sense the recoil in their touch, or a hint of concern in their voice whenever the subject of their children came up in conversation.

But something was amiss with Jair. Although his reactions and words were similar to other Neph parents, there was something in his manner which told him that there was more to this man than meets the eye. Now that he was taking extra time inside the house, he could guess as to what it was.

The twins.

Either Jair was intending on spiriting them away after he returned from helping take Garen home, or worse still, he would instruct them to leave after Jair led Kanias away from the farm, and neither was something that he could allow.

"Master Seraph—," started Garen for the fourth time.

The young Neph's mouth closed with a snap when Kanias turned his bright green gaze upon the boy. "Garen," Kanias said with a growing smile on his face, "I need you to help me with something very important."

Garen sat up straighter and looked upon the Seraph with eager eyes. "Oh yes, yes! Important?"

"Yes, I need you to take the portage trail here the rest of the way home by yourself, and locate Raine and Rennick's mother, Dani. Please tell her to come home."

Garen jumped to his feet. "My mother often sees her at the market," he said, "I will run the whole way!"

The young Neph was already turning to run up the path, but Kanias put a large hand around his wrist and stopped him. "Do not speak to anyone else about this, only the twins' mother." Garen nodded with a big smile. Kanias returned the smile and upon releasing his wrist, the young Neph was off and running up the path.

He watched Garen's little legs carry the boy swiftly up the path. Smiling, Kanias stood up and casually walked off of the lane and toward the thicket that encircled the farm. He would find a less conspicuous spot to watch the farm. He would wait for a little while for Jair to either come out, or for Dani to arrive before approaching the farm. For now, he was hoping that Jair would look out a window and see that he was no longer there, and make the assumption that Kanias had returned with Garen to the village without him. Perhaps it would relax Jair and make the next part a little easier. Either way, he hoped that Garen was as fast as he looked and that Dani was there to receive the message from the boy.

It is much easier to deal with things like this all at once.

Kanias strode into the thicket and melted into the trees.

***

For a moment, it appeared to Rennick that neither he nor Raine dared to even breathe. Their father had just told them of a plan that would not only violate the law regarding Purification, but would virtually assure the fact that they would be hunted down and brought back if captured. In that scenario, it also meant that both Jair and Dani would be subjected to Purification themselves if they were caught.

Jair's mood had shifted from turbulent to subdued, but his demeanor was calm as he charged around their home collecting the things he knew they would need. Occasionally, he glanced out of the side window to spy upon Kanias and Garen waiting for him at the end of the lane.

Their small home consisted of only three rooms that included the main living area with a large rectangular table in the center. There was a hearth on the center of the far wall, with a door on each side leading to the two bedrooms in the rear of the house—one shared by the twins and the other by their parents. After placing the items he had gathered on to the table, Jair opened the door of the twins' room and entered it briefly before reemerging with both of their large traveling packs. He tossed one to each of his children.

"Here," Jair said. His voice was firm and monotone. "Fill these with all of this gear and as much food that you can, I have to take the Seraph back to the village now, but I—." Jair stopped as he looked again out the side window. He peered in several directions before walking over to the other two windows, looking out of each.

Returning from the far window, his face masked in frustration and confusion, Jair walked over to the door, threw it open, stepped a few feet outside and looked over the area. After a minute, he walked back into the house and closed the door.

"What is wrong father," Rennick asked. He sounded like a boy still afraid of the dark.

"Perhaps nothing," Jair responded. "Seraph Kanias and the Larnich boy are no longer at the end of the lane."

"Maybe he just decided not to wait and he took Garen home himself," said Raine hopefully.

Jair said nothing at first. Instead, he just looked at the twins. When he finally spoke, his demeanor took on a completely different tone, his eyes shimmering pools of blue that managed to capture both of the twins with one look. "I am going out to the barn for a moment, then I am going to go into the village to see if I can find your mother. Secure the door and do not let anyone in other than your mother or me inside. And under no circumstance are either of you to leave the house until I return." His voice was slow, soft, and rich. "If I am not back before your mother returns, tell her what has happened, but do not allow her to come find me."

Rennick found himself agreeing almost instantly. There was something strange about Jair's manner, but it seemed like a reasonable request. As he heard Raine agree alongside of him, Rennick believed that he felt his sister recognize the same peculiarity in their father's tone.

Jair took one more look at each of them, glanced out the front window, then opened the door quickly and went outside, closing it behind him. Rennick grabbed the iron bar from the corner next to the door and slid it through the two metal sleeves mounted on each side of the door frame. While Domo Vale always felt safe to Rennick, Jair barred the door each night. His father explained that living on the outskirts of an isolated village comprised of strangers forced to live together may not always be as safe as it appeared. There were never any incidents as far as Rennick knew, but his father seldom left anything to chance.

Raine turned toward the table and began loading gear into her bag while Rennick leaned against the table, watching his father walk across the lane to the barn. He saw Jair grab and light the small lamp beside the door before pushing open the right side of the large, solid oak door of the barn and disappearing inside, leaving the door open behind him.

Doubt and confusion roiled inside of Rennick as he turned his back to the window to face the table where the implements of their doomed escape lay arrayed before him. Opening his pack, he started roughly tossing some of the gear on the table inside of it. Raine, reaching over with a thin, but firm hand, grabbed Rennick's wrist, preventing him from throwing the small lantern he now held into the pack, which would have surely damaged it. Rennick set the lantern down as Raine released her grip.

"Something else is going on that nobody is telling us," Rennick said firmly under his breath.

Raine looked up to meet Rennick in the eye. Her gaze was dark, but steady. Her voice low, but strong. "Perhaps," she said. "But we have to trust Father and do as he says."

"That is the whole problem," Rennick started, before averting his eyes and pressing his balled fists into the smooth wood surface of the table. "I do not want to make matters worse for everybody, simply because I manifested early! If we run away, we will get caught, and then Father, Mother, and you will be punished as well."

"I know, but what other choice do we have?" Raine now placed her steady hand on Rennick's shoulder, and he could feel some of the tension leaving him. She always had a way of calming him, even if she was the source of tension. "Besides," she continued in a confident voice, "Who says that we will get caught? Nobody knows this area better than the four of us."

The confidence in Raine's tone was contradicted by the anxious look in her darkening eyes. She needed to know that she was helping Rennick. Telling Raine that the Seraph had numerous ways to track them, even in unfamiliar wilderness, was not going to make her feel better. So he nodded until it became apparent that he could not remove the worry from his face completely.

"Is there something else," Raine asked.

Rennick sighed. "The Seraph worry me," he replied, "It is obvious that at least Kanias knows what is happening, and he does not appear to be concerned. If anything, he seems pleased, which is dismaying, when I consider the situation. Something is not right."

Raine, appeared to weigh her words very carefully before she responded. "I do not know about the other two Seraph, but as far as Kanias is concerned, I do not see him in the same light as you. In fact, I trust him. There is something about him that makes me feel safe. Whatever he knows, I do not imagine him bringing us any harm."

Rennick did not want to disagree with his sister, as he had felt the same thing. Kanias did seem quite likable, despite his gruff exterior, and he did save them from the river. At the same time, Rennick could not believe that any Seraph would simply ignore one important reality. That Rennick was a Manifested Neph.

Raine's arm shot out past Rennick's chest and pointed to the front window. "Look! Kanias!"

Rennick turned and he saw the brawny Seraph walking up the lane, heading toward the barn. Kanias, glancing over to the window, made Rennick flinch. But the bright day and the dark interior of the house prevented the Seraph from seeing inside. By the time Kanias slowed his pace, he was within a few strides of the open barn door. Upon reaching it, he leaned to look carefully inside. Rennick saw a slow shake of Kanias' bald head, as if the Seraph had seen something that disappointed him and did not make any sense. Taking a deep breath, he stood tall and opened the door wider, before entering the barn and closing it behind him.

"I am going out there," Rennick said, moving toward the barred door.

"Are you crazy," Raine asked, grabbing her brother's shoulder and spinning him around with a force he did not know that she possessed. "Let Father handle it."

Rennick looked out at the barn door, trying to imagine what was happening behind it. When he looked back, he saw a willfulness he had never seen before radiating from the dark, pleading eyes of his sister. His father's earlier directive and Raine's earnest reaction overpowered his impulse as he moved back to Raine's side by the table. Kanias had entered the barn without any weapon, but he was a Seraph, and weapons were not necessary.

Without taking his eyes off of the barn door, Rennick began to place various gear from the table haphazardly into his pack. And then he saw it. All of the moisture left his mouth.

A thin line of smoke rose from the barn's upper window.

"Ren, maybe we should go out there," Raine said in an anxious whisper.

Rennick could not agree more.

Chapter 6: The Honor of One

AS Jair walked out of the house, closing the door behind him, it was difficult for him to not run. But he was sure that the twins were watching him, so he forced himself to walk casually toward the barn. He released a breath he realized he had been holding only after hearing the reassuring thud of the door bar being put into place by Rennick. While it was superficial protection against a Seraph, or any of the other dangers that may now exist for the twins, it was something, and he clung to anything that resembled hope.

Raine and Rennick are Seraph.

That notion changed everything, bringing Jair a new and frightening sense of clarity. All the evidence confirmed this theory, and it made his next actions seem even more vital. Upon hearing Raine's recollection of what occurred at the Pyn, it was apparent to Jair that Kanias was clearly expecting to find a young Seraph by the river. He was also sure that he had witnessed the Seraph Kanias Delving the twins as they left the camp, and discovering something that pleased him a great deal as a result. The twins being Seraph would definitely account for Kanias' reaction. However, Jair was still missing a vital piece of information.

As Jair reached the barn, he approached the unlit oil lamp which sat on the barrel to the right of the door. Then he opened the small squat metal box filled with sand sitting next to it. Using the metal tongs tied to its handle with a braided leather thong, he lifted a hot coal out of the sand.

Raising the glass on the lamp dome, he leaned in and blew on the coal as he held it to the exposed wick. A thin ribbon of red crept over the edge of the coal, and within a few seconds, ignited the oil-soaked wick. Lowering the glass globe, Jair watched the flame grow before lifting the latch on the solid, metal-bound barn door and pushing the right half of the double doors inward.

From the beginning, Jair thought the journey to the very point where he stood, at that exact moment, would be the most difficult of his life. Little did he know. Never would he question the mission put before him. It was not his place. Only to follow through to its end was of any importance. Why else would seeing children raised to their eighteenth Yelta Luna and then properly Purified have been issued as his honor task, his *Gran Shiga*? Nothing was ever assigned as a Gran Shiga to a Cou'Rali Adept unless the task itself was nearly impossible. The realization of his Master's objective was a matter of life or death for him. And others.

When Jair had ascended to the status of Adept by surviving his Winnowing eighteen years before, his Master issued this charade as this honor task. He was a young man suddenly in charge of twin infants. Dani, the other survivor of his Winnowing, was equally puzzled by the task they were commanded to undertake under the guise of husband and wife Neph. Other Gran Shiga entailed such things as assassinations of dangerous individuals or attempting to rise to a position of power. That was the mystery for Jair. He was not sure why the twins were so important, or why he had been instructed to raise them as Neph. Instructions for a Gran Shiga, however, were always followed as dictated, because often it was the only possible way for the particular task to be accomplished. In this case, perhaps knowing less would lend authenticity to the illusion.

Or perhaps the reasons are too dangerous to know.

Jair's orders had been simple: With Dani as his wife, he was to raise the children as Neph. Never tell them the truth. Never allow them be alone with a Seraph. Upon their eighteenth Yelta Luna, he would deliver them for Purification, thus eliminating all risks to their safety and health. Up to that very day, he and Dani had succeeded. Then the Larnich boy fell into the river, possibly rendering years of devotion and sacrifice pointless. Now the Seraph, Kanias, was a threat that required elimination. A thread had come loose and the intricate tapestry that was his honor task could soon be nothing more than a pile of string.

Upon accepting the Gran Shiga, Jair would wonder if the lesson and difficulty of his particular honor task was found in weathering the years of wondering and not knowing its purpose. For Jair, his task became both easier and more difficult on the day he realized that he loved his adopted children as his own flesh and blood. Now he realized that failure to see his honor task through to its end not only meant that he would die, but that the twins and Dani would as well. His death, whenever it would occur, was something that any Cou'Rali was prepared to accept, as long as the task prevailed. But time and circumstance had complicated everything that Jair had once known. To see the death of his two young charges and of the woman he had grown to love, his family, would be a fate worse than his own death to be sure.

Aspects of Jair's training had prepared him for the shame and segregation of Declaring himself a Neph. He was prepared to live for years within that isolation until the day came that the twins were to be Purified. He was even prepared for the mundane burdens of living as a simple farmer raising a family. What he had not been prepared for was the fact that he had grown accustomed to that life. Dani was his wife, a role she played in their elaborate ruse. But he was also her husband in that he loved her. And she loved him. They were joined together with ties stronger than a Gran Shiga. Rennick and Raine were their children. They were a family.

Jair had even grown to love the identity they managed to carve out for themselves in Domo Vale. He dreamed of continuing that life after their Gran Shiga was completed, except this time it would be on his terms. He would have earned it as his reward for success. That dream, as much as anything else, compelled him to enter the barn.

The barn door swung slowly on well-oiled hinges, Jair sliding in between the two halves with little room to spare. He left the door partially open, providing him additional light and a view of the house from the inside. The barn, smelling of their cow, moulder, and hay, had two levels: the main level he was quickly walking across, and an upper loft where hay and other dry goods were stored.

The wide open main level was broken up by several thick support beams and held five open stalls along the right hand wall, one of which was Cassie's. A long, steep ramp ran up from the right side of the rear wall, providing access to the loft floor on the left side. It made it easier to move items up to the loft, especially when they used the three wheeled lift cart which now sat near the double doors.

When Jair built the barn eighteen years before, he had made it so the left side of the ramp was supported by a solid wall. His explanation was that it was necessary for support, but his real purpose was to have an enclosed storage area for tack, tools and other items under the ramp. There were three doors spaced along the wall, each one leading to a small storage closet.

Reaching the end of the ramp, Jair knelt by the lowest section of that wall. That area was too small to be used as an efficient storage area, the nearest closet ending a few feet from where he knelt. A nimbus of light surrounded Jair in the dim barn from the lantern, which he set down carefully by his feet. With all of the windows in the upper loft area still shuttered, the only other illumination came from a small square window located in the center of each wall, and the slightly open barn doors behind him. Producing a small lever from his belt pouch, he pried the third support plank off the wall.

Aside from Dani, everyone else assumed it was just dead, unusable space. Jair had to make sure that everyone believed it was exactly that. So he feathered a *Suggestion* to the twins, as well as Valen Hartel, an old Neph who helped them during planting and harvest, that the space was useless and not worthy of any attention. So they all ignored it. In reality, however, the deceptively large space held several very important items.

He had to be careful when using his Maior talents, like Suggestion, especially in a region filled with Neph. True Neph, and those of other De'Lani, could not feel the use of Lani abilities, but if one who could sense the use of them was nearby, a Seraph for example, the use of Lani in such an area would cut the dark like a lantern in a room with no light. It would certainly to draw attention. Strictly speaking, it was not a crime for declared Neph to use their former Lani powers. It was a matter of honor.

Just the thought of using his Lani power made the bandu on his forehead tingle. It was a reminder of the Spirit Oath he and Dani took in becoming declared Neph. That Oath, accepted by and sealed with the bandu upon their Spirit by a Seraph, would serve as a guide. But it would also punish Jair and Dani if they dared to violate their honor. Break their Oath, and the Oath would break them. It was the same for all declared Neph. But of course it was not that simple for Jair and Dani.

What others did not know was that when he and Dani had accepted the bandu, they were already bound by an even stronger, more important Spirit Oath, their Gran Shiga. Upon accepting their honor task, they were required to do everything necessary, even sacrifice their lives, to ensure success of their honor task. From time to time, that meant violating their bandu. But their Gran Shiga protected their honor, ensuring that their Spirit would neither burn, nor punish them for their lack of honor to the bandu. His and Dani's lives were often a matter playing a dangerous game, one of balancing two independent and often competing Oaths. The fact was that either of the Spirit Oaths had the capacity to kill Jair and Dani at any moment by failing to protect their honor. But it was a balance that they had learned to wield.

It was not a neat or quick death either. Writhing and screaming, some offenders would try to bargain for forgiveness from Erta, but it was never granted. Begging for relief from the torment until the moment dishonor ripped the offender's Spirit from their body was brutal, but it was the punishment for breaking the code of the Cou'Rali.

Honor before life, death before dishonor.

Reaching into the darkness of the space beneath the ramp, Jair carefully drew out a long object wrapped in a coarse burlap sack. Setting it at his feet, he reached once more inside and pulled out a fist-sized pouch. He replaced the slat of wood onto the wall, making sure that it was secure with four quick raps with the wooden handle of the lever.

He first untied the thong at the top of the soft, tawny leather pouch, dumping the contents into his long, calloused hand. There were fifteen pieces of Cha'Li gold, a veritable fortune in their area, and something else even more valuable, Dani's bonded Emerald. One could be used for goods and services in any place in the Realm without question. The other was Dani's link to her own past.

Jair's link to his past lay wrapped in the burlap before him. Placing both the gold and the gemstone back into the pouch and setting it aside, he carefully revealed the hilt of the long sword that lay within.

Gripping the burlap sack to secure the scabbard within it, he gently shook the sword out onto the dirt floor. Rays of light from the lamp glinted off the four feet of metal that made up the straight, double-edged blade. It was the spray of blue color, however, flashing off of his bonded Sapphire at the end of the hilt that made him smile. The color was so intense, providing kindling for his memories from another life, his life before Dani and the twins. Ignoring the tingle of his bandu, he set aside the sack with the scabbard inside and touched the stone. Jair instantly felt whole again. There were larger, more powerful sapphires in existence, but this one was special. It was his.

He reached for his sword, but his hand stopped just short of the leather wrapped hilt. The reality of seeing his sword within reach of his hand without feeling the burn of his bandu, made clear the reality of what had to happen. Gripping the hilt as he stood, Jair not only felt the familiar source of power pressing against the glyph on his wrist, but also the familiar feeling of the worn leather wrapped hilt perfectly matched to the grip of his left hand. They reminded him that the things that made him extraordinary before were not forgotten. The thousands of hours of brutal training. The horrors of his Winnowing. The shocked face of the Seraph, Wyann, as his sword slid through her heart eighteen years ago.

Am I prepared to do that again?

Uncertainty and fear raged within him. Everything had changed that morning, the moment he and Dani realized that Raine and Rennick were both gone. That Cassie was missing as well told Jair that Rennick likely went to the clearing with the rock. It was then that Jair decided to retrieve his son, hoping to find his daughter as well.

Jair played the events over repeatedly in his head. He had encountered Kellen Ohsider on his wagon coming down the portage path from Domo Lake when Jirri and four young Neph came through the trees. Seeing the Seraph made his heart race, and upon hearing the story of what had transpired at the river, he knew who was involved long before the Seraph said anything to him about Raine and Rennick. Eager to get to the twins, he asked Kellen to take the Neph into the village for the Seraph, find Dani, explain to her what happened, and tell her to return to their farm immediately.

Never allow them to be alone with a Seraph.

Yet there they stood, on the banks of the Pyn River on the very last day of his Gran Shiga, with not just one, but three Seraph.

Jair's anger had gotten the best of him at that moment, and Kanias' manner with the twins intensified his anger still further. When he noticed the thin, wiry Seraph grab the staff, however, his priority shifted back to separating the twins from the Seraph. They had all made themselves memorable to the Seraph, Kanias in particular, and that was bad enough. But fighting with three Seraph and being revealed as a Cou'Rali Adept? That would be disastrous. Worse still, Jair was confident that one of the other two Seraph were there to insure that his Gran Shiga was completed. It was likely that all of his actions were being reported, weighed, and measured.

Now that Jair understood that Kanias believed the twins to be Seraph, he had to act. He still felt that he may not have all of the information, but he had taken too long already, and the time for action had come. Jair could neither allow the Seraph to take the twins, nor could he allow them to be Purified, as it would kill Rennick. So he had consigned himself to taking the twins away, knowing full well that such a task would eventually require him to confront Kanias. His mind racing, he tried to think of a way where he would not have to kill the Seraph but still slip quietly away, assuming the role of just another Neph family trying to avoid Purification.

That opportunity, unfortunately, would never be an option. Jair was certain that if they simply disappeared, Kanias would never stop searching for them, using every resource available to collect the twins. It would not be long before most of Natura would be on the lookout for them, making it impossible to escape capture. If that were to happen, there would be no doubt that his Master himself would come and deal with the situation. And in that scenario, no one would make it out unscathed. Not the Seraph, not the twins, and certainly neither Dani nor Jair. A failure of that magnitude of a Gran Shiga? He shuddered at the prospects, and he felt his determination grow.

A change in the light coming from the barn door, and the dull scrape of a hard boot behind him told him that he was not alone. He did not need to look to know who it was. Feeling the presence was enough. Jair felt his honor hardening the growing resolve to act, as he turned to see the broad-shouldered silhouette of Kanias pulling the barn door closed behind him. As the door latch clicked, Jair realized his course of action was decided.

Honor before life, death before dishonor, Seraph.

Chapter 7: Behold My Children

DANI Sherrill walked with long, swift strides down the portage path, heading toward the home she had built with Jair nearly 20 years before. Her mind was clouded with questions, creating a grim pall over her olive skin. The message Jair had sent to her through Kellen Ohsider, telling her about the accident at the river and asking her to hurry back to the farm, was still shaking her typical calm demeanor.

One day left, and this happens.

A young Neph, no more than five-years old, appeared ahead of her on the path, running around a short bend ahead. Seeing the tall Nym, he ran for Dani, waving and smiling with each step.

"Hello, I am Garen," the young boy said as he reached her around deep breaths. "You are Raine's mother, aren't you?"

Despite her mood, Dani had a difficult time keeping a smile off of her lips. "Yes, Garen, my name is Dani," she said, her smile growing. "Have you seen Raine recently?"

"Yes," he replied with a wide grin. "I just left your farm. She is there now with her brother and father. Raine saved me from the river!"

Dani's smile faded a little as she looked over the Neph who had been the source of so much tension this morning. But there was no sense of fear or angst in his voice, so perhaps all was well at the farm, now that Jair had retrieved them.

"The Seraph Kanias sent me to find you," Garen continued as Dani's heart beat a little faster. "He is waiting at the end of your lane. If you hurry, you may still find him there."

"Garen, thank you," she replied. "Now you head straight back to the village and go home. I am sure your mother is anxious to see you."

"Please tell the Seraph Kanias that I found you," said Garen with an eager expression, "And tell him that I did my job!"

"I will," Dani said over her shoulder, as she began striding up the path again.

Garen seemed proud to deliver the message, and Dani tried to give him a rewarding smile, but the shadow that lay over her heart made it little more than flashing her teeth at the young Neph. This message, while nothing more than a summons, did provide her with some good information. First, Jair was with the twins, and they were all together. Second, a Seraph was there as well, watching the farm. Perhaps this Seraph, Kanias, was the one she was seeking. But she could not be certain of any Seraph's motives, in particular when it came to this day. She had to be sure.

Dani and Jair had received a cryptic note during Yelta Luna the year before indicating that someone would be coming to verify the completion of their Gran Shiga. When they discovered today that both of the twins were gone, she and Jair had decided that they were going to split up their effort, with Jair searching for the twins, and Dani going into the village to see if she could learn who may have been sent. Perhaps this individual would reach out before Ceremony, or perhaps only become involved if the task appeared likely to fail.

Either way, both Jair and Dani were convinced that it would be easier if they knew who was watching their efforts. It might become important information as the day went on to know the identity of their hidden ally.

She had wandered through town all morning, the streets and vendors bustling with activity. She hoped that amid all of the visitors arriving for Ceremony from the surrounding area, that one would approach her to declare that they were the subject of the mysterious note. But no one did. There were no notes, no attempts to make contact. Either no one had arrived, no one was coming, or whoever it was would remain hidden until the time was right.

Now Dani found herself in a potentially dangerous situation and lacking in the one resource she considered more valuable than any other. Knowledge. Dani managed to survive her Winnowing and was chosen for this task simply because she gathered, and used, more information than anyone else. It was a skill she had mastered, an art she had perfected. Aside from playing the part of Jair's wife, she was also his eyes and ears. At that moment, however, she felt both blind and deaf. She knew it was time to see and hear again.

Turning off the path, she strode into the trees and began to reach out to her ultimate source of insight and comfort, the plants. Individuals who were not Nym never quite understood how much knowledge the grass, shrubs, and particularly, the trees, gathered and stored. But they also spoke to each other. Carried upon the wind, through the earth, and by every rustle of leaf and branch, plants shared what they knew. They could tell you just about anything that you could possibly want to know about their environment around them, if one chose to be patient enough to just listen.

Slowly, she opened herself to the Lani power that was an inherent part of every Nym. It was the same power to which she had given a Spirit Oath eighteen years before, vowing to never use again. The slight tingle from the bandu upon her forehead vanished as another, older Oath compelled her to continue. She was certain that the only way she could help Jair and the twins survive the next few hours was to learn more about what was happening, and this was her way.

Dani's Spirit, blossoming under the touch of the Lani pulsing through her once again, felt like the sunbaked grass of a hill being caressed with the first cool rain of Autumn. It was dangerous for her to be using her Lani, with not just one, but three Seraph in the area. However, she knew that this was the one way she could gain some advantage again. Time and time again, she had learned that success was as much about having key information, as it were about skill or talent. When Dani had both, she was a powerful force.

The trees in her immediate vicinity put her at ease as they

whispered stories of rain coming upon the west wind. As she walked through the thicket, heading in the direction of their home, she allowed her mind to float on that story as it reached out over the breeze, becoming part of the river of information that always drifted above oblivious heads. She heard stories of creatures, great and small, wandering through the wooded areas. There was also scintilla of fear as the wind carried rumor of an untended fire in the trees not far away on the banks of the river.

Then she felt it. It was like a whirlpool in the river of information. A void, a spot where the trees did not talk, did not whisper a thing. The river of consciousness flowed around it, reached toward it, but did not touch it.

She knew this feeling well. Someone was there, and was commanding the trees to silence. This close to the farm, she concluded, it had to be one of the Seraph, perhaps the one who summoned her. Like the sun dropping behind a cloud, she cut off her connection to the Lani power and hastened her steps toward home. It may not have been much, but at this point there was at least one Seraph was watching her home. Her initial thought was that it was probably the Seraph Kanias, but she would have not made it one day through her Winnowing had she allowed such assumptions to rule her logic.

Dani forged her way through the foliage, traveling roughly parallel to the portage road off to her right. As she neared the farm, she slowed, searching the trees around her, looking for the telltale signs of a foreign presence. Years of living in the woods, combined with her own specialized training allowed her to move silently, without snapping a branch or creating more than a slight rustle in the leaves littering the thicket floor. After a few minutes, she began to see the hint of buildings and grass through the breaks in the trees and leaves.

Rounding a young fir tree, she froze when she saw the Seraph. Dropping slowly to one knee beside the fir, she watched for any sign that her arrival had been noticed.

The large, thick Seraph was standing just inside the edge of the thicket, leaning against a tree and staring into the clearing where Dani's farm stood. He did not show any sign of being aware of her a few strides away. Appearing distracted, he was rubbing the top of his bald head, as if pondering a difficult question. She wondered if this individual was the Seraph Kanias who had sent her the message. He did not look like someone waiting to cause trouble or harm to anyone. If anything, his body language seemed to her to be equal parts interested and worried.

Caution held Dani back, as she did not see anyone else nearby or outside of the house which stood about fifty strides away. She heard the barrel-chested Seraph release a sigh of resignation, and stride out from under the eaves of the thicket toward the farm.

His movement caused Dani to flinch toward him, and she stopped herself. If the twins and Jair were down there, they would certainly greet anyone walking into the midst of the farm, and their reaction would determine her action. The Seraph did not appear to be aware of her, so it might be useful to keep her presence hidden as long as possible. She was confident that Jair could handle one Seraph by himself if it were completely necessary; she had seen him do it before.

The Seraph walked into the courtyard and made his way directly to the barn, which Dani now noticed had its door slightly ajar. He stood there for a couple of moments, looking at something through the opening, before pushing it open further, entering and then closing the large door behind him. A shiver of panic raced through Dani. She had no idea who else was inside the barn, or what they were doing there, but it was not likely a good situation and she could not stand idly by without knowing what was happening.

Rising from her crouch beside the fir tree, she felt a malevolent force lash out at the young tree. Powerfully summoning her own Lani, she attempted to shield the tree from a Word of Command that was being forced upon it. That she could feel the command, but felt neither the wielder's location nor the use of Emerald Lani meant only one thing.

Seraph.

Her shielding was too late as the command raced through the tree. With the sound of cracking limbs and straining wood, the fir keened in agony. It had become like a limber creature, swinging out its lower branches in a broad arch, smashing Dani in the face and chest with a thick, powerful bough and launching her into the air.

Dani felt the air in her lungs escape as her ribs cracked under the weight of the attack, several of the smaller branches on the bough piercing her side. The faded brown tunic she wore offered little in the way of protection, and she felt one of the small branches slide between her ribs and puncture her lung. While it was not the first time that she had been ambushed, Dani had not kept her skills, or body, as sharp as Jair.

Her role was different now. She was a wife and mother. She tended the garden. She raised two children. She was accepted as a paragon of matronly virtue in their integrated Neph society because she had become one of them. No one looking at Dani in Domo Vale would have guessed that the tall, soft Nym was also a Cou'Rali Adept.

But despite years of neglect, the roots established in Dani were too deep to be completely killed by the frost of domestication. Hitting the ground, Dani pulled her legs up into her body and rolled over her shoulder, allowing her momentum to carry her legs over her head. As her feet rotated above her, she shot her legs out and thrust her hands into the ground, catapulting her into the air. Twisting, Dani saw a blur out of the corner of her eye as another tree limb flew past her, smashing deep into the ground where she had been. A killing blow had it connected. Whoever was attacking her was not underestimating her, regardless of her appearance. No, this person knew exactly who she was.

Our hidden watcher?

Landing on her feet, stumbling and gasping for air, Dani was now facing the opposite direction from the farm. Not graceful, but she was alive. She tensed for the attack that she was sure to follow, but it did not come. Scanning the area around her, Dani searched for her assailant, but saw nothing but trees and torn earth where the fir's last attack had smote the ground.

Using her Lani and feeling out around her, the sheer cacophony the assault had caused beat upon her Spirit. The fir behind her was a twisted, broken steeple of kindling, looking like a powerful wind had blown it apart, inexplicably leaving the other trees nearby unscathed. The verdant air was thick with the essence of violence and fear, as the other trees had felt one of their own turn on itself in fulfilling a being's commands, causing its own destruction. Dani's Nym spirit reached out to her friends, and the outrage that poured into the air flowed into her as well. What had been done not only violated the Balance, but it was a desecration of the world that made her whole.

A Seraph, violating The Balance!

The thought sickened Dani, as the very implication told her that short of being in her own Master's presence, she would never be in greater danger. But this was Dani's Gran Shiga, and the honor bonds upon her Spirit strengthened her and became an impetus for action. She was the first line of defense for Jair and the children. It was her duty to ensure their honor task succeeded, whatever the cost.

The thicket hummed with enmity, with leaves and branches shaking in a tempest of impotent rage. Plants did not understand locomotion or movement as beings and creatures did. Nonetheless, they longed to lash out and attack, flaying flesh from bone. But without a Nym to guide them into action, they were paralyzed through lack of understanding. She did not dare try to do it herself, weakened as she was now. Without having a firm target to focus their rage, they would be as likely to turn on her as they would her hidden foe. It was apparent that her attacker was now using Dani's ability against her, as the background noise and emotion rolling off the trees was like camouflage for her enemy, at least while they existed in this blind rage.

Her breath ragged, Dani labored with each inhalation, the wound in her side forcing blood out past her thin fingers as air leaked from her lungs. She realized that she needed to release the Lani, as it was useless to her, and she needed as much of her focus as possible to help her survive this attack.

Letting go of the Lani was like having blanket of silence drop around her. She could still feel the tension in the air, and saw the branches waving in the calm blue sky as if a gale ripped through them, but her head was no longer filled with the sounds of promised torture and certain death. Amid the relative calm, however, was the feeling of a baleful glare upon her. They were the eyes of a hidden predator upon its fatally wounded, yet still dangerous prey, as it patiently waited for it to die. Yes, this individual knew exactly how dangerous Dani could be, which was why it was content to just watch. She felt the seeds of desperation and fear taking root in her heart, the power behind those hidden eyes were draining her of her will to live.

"You might as well come out, Seraph," Dani said through clenched teeth. "You are either working for or against my Master's will.

If it is against His will, then may Erta be with you, for no one else will be."

She tried to make her words sound foreboding and defiant, but instead she spat them out around jags of coughing, sending bright crimson specks of blood onto the leaves and thin grass at her feet. Dani was dying. Stumbling into trees and seeking her adversary, she longed to find her target. Channeling her fear into anger, she envisioned plucking those eyes out like thistles in her well-tended garden on the roof at home.

Falling to one knee, Dani turned. Sitting with an awkward thump against the trunk of a small larch tree, her breathing was a rapid and shallow pant. She was unable to take in full breaths due to the fluid in her lungs. Death was waiting, and its malevolent eyes watched in anticipation. Dani accepted this with grace and resignation. As an Adept, she had courted death as a reminder of the order of things. Now, she only hoped that in her death, she could help secure the lives of those she loved.

Pulling in the Lani again, she fell willingly into the current of anger and fear that flooded that section of the thicket. It carried her away, as if she were no more than a twig on a stream. Mustering every bit of consciousness and physical power that remained in her broken body, she prepared herself for one last sending to the trees. Her thoughts were scattered by the violent power of a Suggestion, which rose above the tumult of the forest around her, commanding Dani to look towards her home. She obeyed. In spite of her narrowing vision, she saw thick lines of dark smoke rising up from the barn.

Fire.

All hope abandoned her. She knew what was hidden in the barn. The unseen eyes smiled inside her mind, mocking her inability to protect those she loved. They accused her of failing as a true Adept, chiding her for her vain efforts to defeat those who remained vigilant and strong, not allowing themselves to wither and become fruitless as she did. Finally, they taunted her with visions of a painful death for the twins, never her true children, but children she loved like her own.

She knew the words well, but they were not coming to her of her own free will. "Honor before life. Death before dishonor." The eyes she could not see forced the sacred refrain of the Cou'Rali into her mind, shrieking and whispering at once.

Tears filled Dani's eyes as she looked upon the burning barn, the symbol of both her new life and hidden past, being consumed before her. With her last bit of strength, she drew a final breath, not flinching when she felt a vine creeper slide slowly over her shoulder and twirl itself around her neck. Dani accepted its tightening embrace, relishing in the sweet release it offered.

I wish that I could see the twins one more time.

While the light left her eyes, Dani saw Raine and Rennick exit their house, rushing toward the barn. They were silhouetted against the smoke and flames as they beat at the closed door. Dani did not know why, but as her world grew cool and dark, she felt fear burning in those unseen eyes. Fear of the twins. As peace washed over her at last, the final moment of her consciousness was triumphant.

Behold my children.

Chapter 8: Through the Fire and Flames

KANIAS waited as long as he dared before he left the protective cover of the thicket. Just as he began to move, however, Jair emerged from the house alone. With the authority of a man of conviction, he walked across the yard to the barn and entered. Jair was a mystery to Kanias, and each passing moment made the Seraph more anxious.

Perhaps Kanias' decision to disappear from the lane had pushed Jair to take his time in the house, giving the illusion that he was going about his everyday business. Perhaps. There was, however, a stiffness in Jair's casual gait that seemed forced, a common trait in those who try to convince themselves that they are calm and composed when they are, in truth, churning beneath the surface. It looked suspicious, making it clear to Kanias that Jair was not making a trip to the barn for some hay.

The fact remained that Kanias was running out of time. At any moment, Tarien would arrive with the Sherrill cow. Kanias did not know the young Seraph well. In actuality, he had met both Tarien and Jirri only moments before leaving Cha'Li. This was the first Yelta Luna outside of the Temple for the two young Seraph, and it was Kanias' job to make clear what was expected of them in the outside world.

Something about Tarien's manner earlier told Kanias that he might be a bit too eager to remind the beings of Natura that the Seraph were Erta's Chosen, and as a result were never to be questioned. The way Tarien reacted to the emotional Jair previously, and to the subject matter at hand, could very well be the worst possible combination. It told Kanias that something was not right, and could very well lead to something unfortunate that he would prefer to avoid altogether.

And then he felt it, his eyes widening as he sensed the pull of Nym Lani being used some distance to the northwest of him. Kanias felt the pull of the energy through him almost as abruptly as he felt the presence of a Seraph to the north of him, also wielding Nym.

Tarien? No. I felt him to the southeast, walking with the Sherrill cow only a moment ago. Not Tarien. Jirri.

Kanias had given Jirri instructions to stay at the camp until he returned, on the off chance that any villagers sought them out after the mishap at the river. The last thing that Kanias wanted was for nervous and nosy Neph to ask ill-timed questions, certainly not while he had pressing business to attend to with the Sherrill twins.

Alarming him, the Nym ability he initially felt evaporated. The Seraph responsible was not only maintaining a hold on the power, but also moving toward a new location before that Lani winked out as well. Jirri, as a Seraph, would likely investigate the use of any Lani power she sensed in a Neph society. Then Kanias wondered if the user was Dani. Her name suggested that she was a Nym, but Kanias could not be certain. There was too much going on, and he felt his time draw shorter by the second.

Kanias, rubbing the top of his shaved head, pondered what Jair could be doing in the barn, considering a variety of possibilities. After a few moments of deliberation, however, he decided that he could wait no longer. He could feel things begin to unravel, and he needed to regain control as quickly as possible. It was dilemma that he had to assess and rectify immediately. His first order of business was to confront Jair and let him know the details of their situation.

I have found the Realmwalker and her Successor. Here, in Domo Vale.

It sounded ridiculous, but it was true. Kanias needed to impart this to Jair. But he needed to calm him first, and perhaps enlist his aid in getting the twins back to the Temple.

Resigned as to what lay ahead, Kanias entered the area of the Sherrill farm between the house and the barn, looking toward the family's humbly appointed home. He could see himself reflected in the wide pane of glass that was the front window, but sensed more than his own reflection. The stare of two sets of eyes, each pair nearly identical to the other, pierced the glass and focused their intensity in his direction.

Perhaps they will stay put while I am speaking with their father.

Kanias deliberated every step as he approached the open door of the barn, as he wanted to be careful not to startle Jair. In such a situation, the element of surprise was often dangerous if not fatal. Leaning his head carefully around the door, he peered inside. The Seraph's pupils dilated so fully that they absorbed the surface his irises. Even so, he could not believe his eyes.

Jair stood with his back to the door, staring at a long sword in his left hand, a brilliant sparkle of deep blue flashing off a large Sapphire set in the pommel. Kanias was captivated by the sight as it was as astounding as it was unusual. The form of the sword, the posture by which the man stood at that moment, and the fact that Jair lived in a Neph community—holding both a sword and a Sapphire—meant only one thing.

Jair is Cou'Rali.

Kanias clearly recognized the potential danger that not only he was in, but the twins as well.

Is it his Gran Shiga to kill the twins, murdering the Realmwalker and her Successor if they were ever discovered?

At that moment, Kanias discerned inarguably that he needed to confront Jair, to talk to the man and learn the nature of his honor task in order to determine if he was a friend or foe. More importantly, Kanias needed to ascertain the identity of Jair's Master. It was impossible for this to be a matter of coincidence. That is, to find the Realmwalker and Successor as the twin children of a Cou'Rali Adept was oddly convenient and highly unlikely.

Kanias took a deep breath and lengthened his posture as he pushed open the door slightly and walked into the barn. He did not want the twins involved, but he desired even the faintest warning should

Tarien return with the cow. The creak of an old barn door would provide just that, so he turned and closed it behind him.

Turning back toward the place where Jair had been standing, he found himself staring directly into the Neph's eyes. They were jet black, indicating that this Maior, this Cou'Rali in disguise, was near manic with emotion.

Kanias saw his own death mirrored in that glassy stare.

"Jair—," Kanias began, but the words were squelched by two nearly simultaneous uses of Nym ability just beyond the barn. One was the Seraph he had sensed previously while the other was a Nym.

Kanias paused, a small flash of doubt flying across his face. He knew something terrible was happening in the vicinity. With the twins in the house, he had to make sure they were safe.

"I need—," Kanias began. But the Seraph could say not another word as Jair, in one smooth motion, swept up the small oil lamp with his foot, caught it, and flung it at him with force like he had never seen. As soon as the improvised projectile left Jair's hand, he then readied the sword and charged across the dirt floor toward Kanias.

Time slowed. As Kanias watched both the lamp and Jair advance upon him, he knew that he had met his match in the strong, athletic Maior, especially if he was not going to counter Jair's attack. To engage Jair would defeat his purpose. Fighting a Cou'Rali was problematic, as every Cou'Rali Adept considers his or her life the ultimate resource. The most dangerous of opponents, the Cou'Rali fighting style is formed from years of the most inconceivably difficult training, all with the understanding that reaching the definitive goal is often more valuable than the Adept's own life.

Kanias could see the flame fluttering on the exposed wick of the lamp, the oil sloshing in little waves in the glass base. He knew that there would be no way for him to safely handle the lamp and simultaneously protect himself from the advancing Jair. The best defense Kanias could manage would be deflecting the lamp to the dirt floor, and hope that it did not catch the walls of the barn on fire.

Stepping to the left and swatting at it, Kanias angled the lamp toward the floor. Satisfied with the result, he then turned his attention to Jair, who was now leaping through the open area of the barn that lay between them. Using D'ware, Kanias moved at three times the speed of Jair. He had the ability to move faster than that, but it would render him unable to communicate effectively with his opponent. He had to convey to Jair the importance of the twins' role in their world. And he had to learn who the Cou'Rali's Master was. It was a matter of principle.

"Jair, I am not your enemy," Kanias said, sidestepping to the left to the point that he was out of reach of the falling Jair and more importantly, Jair's sword. His words were deliberate and clear so that they would be understood by the Maior.

Despite how fast Kanias was moving in relation to Jair, the dark eyes of the twins' father never strayed from the spot right below Kanias' ribcage. He was a deadly weapon focused upon his target, not to be dissuaded by the feints or misdirection of any one, at any speed. With almost impossible agility, Jair pushed off one of the nearby support beams to redirect his course in midair.

Kanias applauded the Maior's grace and dexterity as he planned his next strategy of defense against him. With no time to spare, he dove beneath Jair to avoid the slash of his sword just as the lantern shattered and blossomed into a blaze on the floor to the right. The splash of the lamp's oil was much greater than Kanias anticipated, creating dollops of fire that now clung to the door of the barn. He needed to end their fight quickly and efficiently, as he could still feel the use of Lani ability outside of the barn. He was still desperate to gain Jair's trust, but the Seraph's attention and allegiance were divided.

"Listen to me Jair," Kanias said. The tone of his voice was similar to the soft roar of the rising flames. "I know that you are Cou'Rali! But I need you to understand that Raine and Rennick are more important than you may have realized. One of them is the Realmwalker!"

Kanias watched Jair land with an easy bounce and spin to face him.

"It does not matter who they are, Seraph," Jair said, "You stand between me and my honor. I will not give them to you, and you will not take them. Only one of us is leaving this barn."

Jair's words were apt and concise, but Kanias could see conflict in the man's eyes. He charged at the Seraph again, this time in a zigzag pattern across the floor, typical Cou'Rali footwork used against those who applied time compression abilities in battle. The goal was to make a D'ware rival, or in this case, a Seraph using D'ware abilities, uncertain about where the Adept was going to attack.

He loves the twins, yet he is bound by honor. He must kill me for knowing their true identities.

"It does not have to be this way," Kanias replied. He continued to circle a support beam in order to keep the Adept at a distance. "Reveal your honor task and who gave it to you. Perhaps we can find a way to help each other."

Jair, darting around the beam, lunged toward the Seraph with a series wide arching slashes of his blade, each time pushing Kanias further toward the row of stalls that ran along the side of the barn. Kanias did not want to pen himself in, so he attempted to shorten his retreat, which meant coming dangerously close to Jair's sword. Even at nearly three times the speed of the Cou'Rali Adept, Kanias was vastly outmatched in hand-to-hand combat. He could speed up and attempt to subdue the man, but it would not resolve his dilemma.

I need Jair on my side!

Glancing over Jair's right shoulder, Kanias saw the flames grow in size and intensity, engulfing that entire wall of the barn. It was then that Kanias became aware that the Nym's use of power was gone and the Seraph's Lani use evolved from D'ware into Maior.

Jair seemed to notice this as well, and a deep snarl crossed his face.

"One of your Seraph pawns is using Lani abilities nearby," Jair said. "If you thought that you could delay me in here while someone steals my children away, you are mistaken."

Kanias had years of Cou'Rali training from many of the premier D'ware Masters in the Realm. He had his share of mock fights against many opponents, both armed and unarmed, in a variety of environments and in an array of styles. But until that very moment, Kanias had never before had to fight for his life. In fact, in all of his years of service, Kanias had never suffered more than a few bruises and a scratch. His station as a Seraph was the ultimate deterrent for any prospective opponent, however threatening. No one intentionally fought a Seraph. Yet here was a man who not only sought to engage him in battle, but was attacking him with reckless abandon.

He doesn't have anything to lose.

The assault between them was both mental and physical. Kanias could hear Jair's voice in his head, telling him that he, a Seraph, was weak. He whispered that Kanias' skills were no match for those of a true Adept. Then a Suggestion from Jair blasted into his head. If Kanias truly wanted Raine and Rennick to be safe, they would certainly be safer in the hands of a mighty Cou'Rali warrior who loved them as his own children.

Give up. Surrender.

Kanias had to drop his grip on D'ware in order to guard himself against the raw power of the Suggestion. Kanias slammed a mental block on the viper-like Maior, while taking a moment to recover from the lurching forward motion of time, to readjust to its normal linear rhythm.

The growing clouds of acrid smoke burned Kanias' eyes as Jair swung the sword overhead with his left hand and grabbed at something hanging on a nearby wall with his right. Kanias slid and rolled to his right, desperate to reach the more open center of the barn. The sword clanged loudly as it struck the dirt floor mere inches from Kanias' left thigh.

Nimbly catching his feet beneath him and bolting upright, Kanias felt a flash of pain in his right leg. A line of crimson edged a tear in his leggings where a small knife sailed by slashing him before sticking with a thud onto the wood of the ramp below. Only Kanias' ability to roll directly to his feet prevented him from taking the knife in the head or chest. The Adept had underestimated the Seraph's agility, but he was sure the Maior would not make that mistake again.

Amid the commotion, Kanias heard a thunderous pounding. It was the twins beating on the outside of the door, the inside wrapped in flames. Facing it, he saw tongues of orange and red feeding hungrily at the floor of the loft and filling the entire lower level with dark smoke.

"Raine and Rennick," Jair yelled over the rumble of the fire. "Do not open the door!" Jair's voice was commanding, rising over the growing sound of popping wood and crackling flames. "The door is on fire! Watch out for the other Seraph!"

The pounding stopped. Kanias did not need to feel the use of Maior to know that Jair had used Suggestion.

Jair's eyes were inky pools of black rimmed with reflected fire. Kanias saw the truth. The Seraph was going to die, even if it meant that Jair would simply stand there and prevent him from leaving until the barn fell on top of them both.

Still holding the mental block in place, Kanias knew he was trapped. Unable to hold D'ware, he had no chance of escaping an armed Cou'Rali. Jair was a lethal adversary, especially since he would fight at all costs. A trickle of blood down Kanias' right leg was a reminder of how narrow of a margin he truly had, if he ever had one at all.

But Jair was pressed for time as well. Uncertain as to what was occurring beyond the doors of the barn made both of their needs pressing. Kanias needed to leave and would likely die trying. Jair needed to leave, and would kill to do it.

Jair charged once more, the sword trailing behind him in his left hand. He crouched and spun while taking three long strides toward Kanias. The Seraph instantly recognized the pattern, although he had never seen it done before with a sword. Bare-handed, it could be deadly. With a sword, it would kill easily and without question.

Time to take a chance.

Releasing Maior, Kanias snatched at the D'ware Lani and slowed time.

Jair's sword was within striking distance now. Spinning and rising toward the Seraph, there was gleam of fire in Jair's eyes. There was no dodging to the left or right for he would not clear the sword. There was no coming inside of the sword's range of motion, which was the closest thing to a defense. Jair's right hand guarded his front well, and he had only one moment to act before he had to drop the D'ware for Maior protection once more.

The only way was to move up and behind himself, onto the ramp.

Leaping vertically, and then horizontally, Kanias felt the slice of the blade's first three passes slide just below his tucked legs, the second of which flashed just inches below his eyes. At that point, he hoped that he had judged the distance correctly.

With sure feet, Kanias landed without a sound, his back hard up against the wall, standing about a third of the way up the ramp built into the back wall of the barn. As soon as he landed, however, he felt the tip of Jair's sword tear through the front of his left leg, cutting through his leather leggings and then his skin, flesh, and, muscle in a slow inexorable manner. The pain in Kanias' thigh was magnified by the slowness of time. However, it passed quickly as he slammed back into real time and placed the mental block on Jair once again.

Jair's frustration was obvious as he gathered himself to leap upon the ramp. Kanias, reeling from time disorientation and pain, wheeled and ran up the ramp, attempting to place some distance between he and the Cou'Rali, hoping that he could reach a window and escape. Perhaps the twins could stop their father, reason with him. But for that to happen, he had to get to them first.

Reaching the loft did not help matters. The floor on the opposite side was already engulfed in flames. The fumes and heat from the fire were palpable, more intense on the upper level than they were below. Kanias was running out of alternatives.

Hearing Jair charging up the ramp, Kanias spied a large door on the opposite wall and ran for it, hoping that he would at the very least survive the fall.

But halfway across the floor, Kanias recognized that he had made a mistake. What lay beneath his feet was already unstable from the flames consuming what was the ceiling below. Exasperated, he turned to see Jair jumping over the last part of the ramp and running across the loft. His legs didn't seem to touch the ground.

"Jair! Stop!" Kanias pleaded with the man, who was neither his friend nor his enemy.

The shredding sound of parched wood and splintering beams resounded throughout the barn, the entire loft floor tilting inward toward Kanias. As large rent opened in a wide half-circle before him, Kanias saw Jair gather himself for what would be a colossal leap across the chasm. But just as he was about to jump, a great burst of flame and smoke rose from the ground upward, instantly igniting the hay falling from the loft to the floor below. Everything collapsed and Kanias lost sight of Jair.

The Seraph pushed himself into the front corner of the barn, distancing himself as far from the chasm as possible. The heat of the flames beating at him, his lungs choked with smoke, he was limited as to what he could do next. It was then that from the shadowy heat before him that a dark figure shot through the flames like an arrow flying to meet its target. It was Jair.

But his thirty foot leap would not be enough.

It was instantly evident to Kanias that Jair was not leaping to save himself; he was leaping to see his target one last time. Cutting through the dense curtain of smoke with his tireless body, Jair threw his sword with deadly accuracy at the stunned Kanias before crashing into the edge of the chasm.

With no time to spare, Kanias used D'ware Lani to slow time again. He deflected the sword, forcing it down and away while he lunged toward the chasm at the falling Adept. Moving as fast as he dared on the unstable remnants of the loft, he managed to grab Jair's right hand, as he heard the sword bounce off what remained of the floor behind him.

Jair's clothing was on fire, and Kanias' own clothing was beginning to smolder as the fire raged around them both. The Maior looked up at the Seraph, his burned face deeply gouged and scored on the left side from slamming into the burning edges of the wooden planks. Kanias released D'ware. His body trembled as he struggled to hold the hand of the man who just tried to kill him moments before, but Kanias was determined not to let go.

"Give me your other hand Jair," Kanias said. "No one needs to die today!"

Jair's face melted from rage into acceptance. "Let me go, Seraph," he said. "I have failed."

"You have not failed—," Kanias began, but a shudder from the floor beneath their combined weight told him only seconds remained to pull Jair to safety. Kanias glanced around frantically. Everything was enveloped by smoke and fire and at any moment, the rest of the barn was going to collapse.

Raine and Rennick Sherrill are the Realmwalker and the Successor!

Kanias remembered the purpose of his confrontation with Jair. Focusing on that, he looked through what remained of the barn's north wall and saw the twins. He wondered if Raine and Rennick, trapped by Jair's Suggestion, would be helpless witnesses to the final phase of the barn's demise, a heart-wrenching prospect to be sure, especially in light of the day's events. What the Seraph saw, however, made him feel like he was the helpless witness.

On the other side of the lane, the Seraph Tarien was holding Raine around the neck as Rennick circled them in confusion. The noise of the collapsing wall had drawn the attention of all three pairs of eyes toward the barn. Kanias saw a smug glee rise in his fellow Seraph's eyes as clouds of fear and anguish intensified around the twins. It was as though Tarien took pleasure in the fact that Raine was his captive and Kanias was incapable of doing anything at all to help her.

Kanias could see that Raine and Rennick were tormented by the sight of Jair's dire predicament growing along with the flames devouring the family's barn. Further up the lane, he saw Jirri emerge from the thicket at the side of the road, a glow of victory proudly displayed upon her face. Kanias was not sure where her allegiances lay, but he had no doubt that they were not where his own rested.

The Seraph looked down upon Jair, who, upon seeing the scene in the lane himself, combined with the look on Kanias' face, finally understood he was with an ally.

"Let me go, Kanias," he said with the resignation of a warrior who had accepted defeat. "I am too damaged to aid you in your cause and it will only delay you if you try to save me." Jair inhaled to speak again but he coughed instead, flecks of blood spraying upon their hands.

The smoke had thickened around them to the point that he could no longer see anything but Jair silhouetted by the flames below him.

"Please, save my children," the broken Adept said, his voice strained and urgent.

At that moment, a thunderous crack came from the supporting beam below Kanias as it failed, pitching him backwards and forcing him to lose his grip on Jair. The barn's remaining framework shuddered and the floor caved in upon itself, falling inward toward the barn floor.

Kanias' strong hands sought something to hold to prevent his fall, but to no avail. The burning wreckage clutched at Kanias with fiery fingers, intent on pulling him into its deadly inferno. As he plummeted toward the ground, the unrelenting cries of Raine and Rennick Sherrill assaulted the Seraph's ears while a powerful sending of Jair's Maior Lani rang in his mind at the same time.

As Kanias landed on the barn's dirt floor in a heap of flesh and bones—mere refuse amid the other chaos and destruction raining down about him—his world went dark. It was only then that the Seraph realized that his own life had meant something, that he had a purpose.

I found the Realmwalker.

Chapter 9: Manifestations

IT only took a second for Rennick to unbar the door, open it, and run to the barn with Raine right on his heels.

"Father," he screamed. He felt both frightened and empowered at the same time.

"What is happening?" Rennick heard Raine echoing him with calls to her father as well. Their voices were in tandem.

Raine and Rennick could feel the heat of the fire warm their skin through their clothes. The entire front of the barn was now smoking, filling the small clearing with a dense, gray haze. The flames within the modest building licked around the sides of the door and around the small window above.

"Raine and Rennick," Jair said to the twins. "Do not open the door!" Jair's voice was muffled, yet determined and carried easily over noise of the flames. "The door is on fire! Watch out for the other Seraph!"

Of course, they would do as Jair requested. He was their father.

Raine and Rennick obeyed and backed away from the door. The fire had already blackened the lower portion of the barn. They assumed that Jair and the Seraph Kanias were attempting to extinguish the flames from inside so they could exit the barn, and that they just wanted them to move out of the way for their own safety.

Rennick remembered that one of the other Seraph would be

arriving shortly with Cassie, so Jair would naturally want them to keep an eye out for the visitor. It all made sense in his head, but there was a voice nagging at him in the back of his mind, trying to be heard. He looked over at his sister, and could see her nodding in agreement. But there was a dark, confused look in her eyes. Something was not adding up for Raine either. But they followed the wishes of their father nonetheless.

Rennick looked up the lane where he saw the tall, lanky form of Tarien walking just behind Cassie, the brown cow ambling toward the clearing as she always did. Tarien appeared to note the smoke in the air and the agitation in the twins, but did not quicken his pace. Instead, his eyes were flickering about as if he were looking for someone.

Raine hurried up the lane toward the Seraph Tarien, and was beginning to impart the news that their father and Kanias were trapped in the burning barn when he looked toward her in a way that made Rennick uncomfortable. She stopped. A thin smile, devoid of any warmth, broke across Tarien's normally neutral expression. The smile never reached his eyes, however, which radiated contempt as he regarded Raine.

Rennick only caught the slightest tension building in Tarien's stance before the Seraph was running up the lane in a blur of gray and green toward his sister, who appeared rooted in place. The Seraph flashed by Cassie, and the cow observed him with a wary eye.

Rennick saw the danger and ran, moving up the path toward the clearing. As he increased his speed, he noticed the pain in his side from earlier in the day. He was closer to Raine than was the Seraph, but was running much slower. He did not know what Tarien was going to do, but Rennick was certain it would not be good.

With an additional burst of speed, Tarien reached Raine first and quickly wrapped two long arms around her, pulling her arms back at the elbows with one arm, and holding her at the neck with the other. Raine struggled, trying to wriggle herself free, but Tarien's arm muscles rippled with effort, and he squeezed her even more closely to his body. A look of fear and helplessness leapt from Raine's black eyes to her brother's, her breath rasping through her lips as she tried to call out his name.

"Raine," Rennick shouted. "I am coming."

Rennick had seen his sister in trouble before, many times, but he could not recall ever seeing true fear in her face before. Not like this.

To see it now paralyzed his heart. Grabbing his belt knife seemed like a foolish gesture. For some reason, however, it made him feel better to have something in his hand as he approached Tarien, for the contempt in the silent Seraph's eyes spoke volumes.

Rennick slowed to a stop about five feet from the Seraph and his sister, his arms outstretched, making soothing noises as if he were trying to calm a gray-lined bear he had unintentionally disturbed.

"What is wrong, Seraph Tarien," Rennick said slowly. "Why are you doing this?"

But before the Seraph could answer, a loud rumble erupted from the barn behind them. He turned to look. Raine and Tarien followed. Together they watched as one side of the barn fell into two pieces, crumbling to the ground in a matter of seconds.

In the distance, in the middle of the loft floor centered over one of the main supports of the barn, Rennick saw Kanias holding Jair above the burning debris, his father's leggings on fire. The rising heat shimmered around them. Rennick watched his father say something to Kanias, then turn and look straight at Rennick. Even from that distance, Jair's eyes filled Rennick's mind with the sound of his enduring, sometimes impatient voice.

A loud crack came from the support beam as it fell away, pitching Kanias backward and behind the falling floor, breaking his grip on Jair's wrist in the process. The timber split and splintered into a sharp point, jutting upward just as Jair was falling.

Rennick shrieked as he watched the beam pierce his father's chest through his back. A dark spout of almost black blood bursting from both the wound and from Jair's open mouth. His father's head jerked around until his dark eyes met with Rennick's own, filling the boy's mind again. This time, the voice Rennick heard, Jair's voice, was commanding, but reassuring.

Rennick! Trust Kanias. He knows who you are. No longer safe. Beware Shadowman. Take care of Raine. Find your mother. I loved you like a son—

Rennick cried out as another grating crack struck the air. It was followed by the remaining walls tumbling inward, disintegrating on top of Jair and Kanias. It sent a large cloud of dirt and sparks billowing above the place where the barn once stood. The planks and timbers that comprised the roof were now nothing more than a mound of burning rubble.

"Father!" Rennick was certain his voice made no noise other than a coarse cry that rang in his ears.

I loved you like a son.

Rennick stumbled toward the pile of smoldering ash that was the family's barn, where he and Raine played as children.

Take care of Raine!

The words carried on his father's voice moments before stabbed at him over and over. He heard his sister whimper as he spun around to face the Seraph who held her locked in his arms. Raine's eyes were wild, dark and outlined in red as she struggled to keep her legs firm beneath her. Tarien embraced her in an awkward position making it difficult for her to stand.

Rennick's voice trembled as he spoke, his words weighed down with emotion.

"Master Seraph, please let her go. We did not do anything wrong." Rennick knew his plea was in vain, later confirmed when he saw Seraph Jirri approach Tarien from behind.

They're working together!

Rennick tensed with the knife in his hand, unsure as to what he would do with it exactly, waiting for Jirri to make her move.

Jirri locked eyes with Rennick when she reached Tarien. She ran her hand up her visibly tense comrade's back, her long fingers caressing his spine beneath his tunic. She whispered softly in Tarien's ear, and his muscles noticeably slackened. Her hand then glided over his left shoulder, and trailed down his arm. She stopped to cup Raine's chin in her palm. Jirri's other hand gently pulled Tarien's arm away, allowing Raine to stand on her own.

Raine scrubbed at her eyes with her fingers, and then looked over at Rennick who could not look away from the place where the barn once stood.

Jirri spoke. "I apologize for Tarien's rough handling, Raine. But we could feel that Kanias was in danger, so we acted urgently, not knowing what to expect." Jirri glanced casually at the barn. A strange gleam in her eye as she appraised the burning building. "He just did not know what was happening exactly, who was with him and who was against him. Do you understand?"

The Seraph Jirri's tone was less than sincere.

"I understand," Raine said. "But we need to check on my father and Seraph Kanias," Her neck was already bruised and her voice raspy from Tarien's headlock. She began walking toward the barn.

Jirri's thin, but strong, hand caught Raine by the arm and stopped her. "I am sorry, but they are gone, and we need to leave now." The Seraph said this in a matter-of-fact tone that made Rennick's stomach churn.

"That was our father," Rennick retorted. His anger took hold of his tears. "And the life of someone who saved our lives just hours ago. We need to look for them, and if they are dead, honor them properly."

A rush of bravery Rennick had never felt before coursed through his body. He did not care if the Seraph Jirri took offense. He was either going to die during Purification or run away with Raine, so it seemed futile to concern himself with what a Seraph thought about anything at that point, especially when it came to the matter of honoring their father.

Tarien stiffened, so Jirri released Raine in order to put a soothing hand on the wiry Seraph's shoulder. Nothing had changed about Tarien's posture, but the look in his eyes told Rennick that Jirri was holding him at bay for now. The combination of her cold composure and Tarien's scarcely held restraint, not unlike that of a pet wolf, had Rennick feeling even more anger and resentment than he did previously. Jirri was in control, but what Tarien had done to Raine infuriated him. Even Cassie, who had stopped to eat some grass a few feet away, appeared to eye Tarien with open disdain. Something was not right.

Raine turned to look at Jirri, her eyes large and dark. The two locked gazes for what seemed like hours, entwined in a mental arm wrestling match. They stared stone-faced for a few moments until Raine gasped, her eyes going as black as Rennick had ever seen them. The skin around them tightened, and he could feel her very presence as surely as he felt the heat from fire that had consumed their barn. Rennick had never sensed Raine's existence so intensely before, her life mixed with his own to the point that where they began and ended was indeterminable. Rennick could hear his sister's mind without her uttering a word. He felt her impressions and feelings even though the actual words were sometimes muffled or confused. It was as if Rennick were listening through a wall of emotion, Raine on the other side speaking only to him.

And he could feel her rage. At murder, burning hot. And a freezing sadness for Jair and Dani.

Jair and Dani?

Rennick had never heard Raine refer to either of their parents by their names before. It was struck him as odd until those thoughts were swept away by a surge of regal power that flooded out of Raine and into their two visitors.

Raine's eyes bloomed into bright pools of blue as a smile grew upon her face. Time appeared to stop. Conversely, Jirri's breath hissed slowly through her clenched teeth as the color in her face drained away. Her scream was silenced only by the trembling of her lips. Rennick saw movement to his left for the first time since the staring began. It was Tarien. He was watching Jirri and Raine as well, a look of awe and horror searing through the severe angles of his face. Raine was his focus, however.

Rennick observed Raine as she stood more upright, her infinitely blue eyes framed by a tangle of long dark hair, some strands still clinging to bits of mud and leaves from their earlier river adventure. Rennick's mind, however, saw his sister as Jirri's mind did—tall and beautiful, her hair a cascade of brown silk tumbling gently over proud shoulders. Raine's features were as striking as they were strong, nothing short of stunning. Small points of blue light seemed to radiate from Jirri, but they winked out as they approached the aura of white emanating from Raine.

Jirri broke eye contact with Raine, and the vision as well as the light guttered out. The world appeared to wobble for several seconds while Rennick swayed in a state of momentary vertigo.

Raine beheld Jirri with a sense of revelation in her eyes as the female Seraph lowered her gaze. Rennick noticed that Jirri appeared to shrink away from his sister, as if Raine had threatened her. But Raine had said nothing. As his sister spun to look at Rennick with amazement blooming upon her face, Rennick saw Jirri flash her eyes toward Tarien. It seemed as though Jirri mentally whispered to Tarien, and then let go of him as if she were pinching the flame of a candle to extinguish it.

Tarien's eyes narrowed.

"Rennick! I— I mean we," Raine stammered. "We are not Neph," There was a joyous ringing in her voice. "We are—," Raine began, but she did not finish.

There was a flash of motion where Tarien had been standing. He was a snarling arrow streaking toward Raine, intent and full of purpose. Tarien wore his mission like a mask, not to capture, but kill.

Rennick moved to intercept Tarien, but just as he took a step to intervene, their cow Cassie, charged into the path of the Seraph, catching Tarien on the hip and sending his lanky form spinning to the ground. The look on Tarien's face morphed from surprise to anger as he skidded to a stop a few feet from the cow. He was trying his footing when Cassie bounded after him, rearing then firing a succession of cutting kicks into Tarien's head and body. He attempted to shield himself with his arms and hands, but the animal's hooves continued to find their mark, raising half-moon slashes of red where they met the Seraph's skin. The attack was relentless.

Rennick watched in horror as the cow stomped the Seraph to death. He looked up at Raine, and saw that she was neither horrified nor surprised. There was a sense of justice and satisfaction emanating from his sister. She looked up, meeting Rennick's eyes.

Raine's face softened when she saw the panic and dismay on her brother's face.

"We do not have to be afraid anymore," she said.

As Raine turned and walked toward Jirri, Rennick said nothing. The Seraph's face was white with fear as she watched the cow slow her trampling of the broken body that once was the mighty Seraph Tarien. When Raine neared her, Jirri stood up and ran for the trees, cries of terror flying from her mouth.

"Jirri," Raine said in a firm, authoritative command, "Stop." Rennick could feel the potency of his sister's authority, a sense of absolute power, and now Raine was pressing it upon Jirri.

The Seraph halted without hesitation, her face etched with dread. Peering with fearful eyes over her shoulder toward Cassie, Jirri watched as the cow wandered away from the torn, blood-soaked earth silhouetting Tarien's lifeless body. Once away from the carnage, Cassie lowered her head and clipped off a mouthful of grass with her velvet brown muzzle. Although her face was flecked with spots of blood, she behaved as if nothing unusual had happened.

"Now, Seraph," Raine said to Jirri, "You will judge yourself."

Rennick felt the words force their way into the young Seraph's mind. She attempted to resist, but she was helpless against the authority in Raine's voice.

Jirri's face contorted in fear as she turned and marched to a young larch tree at the edge of the clearing where she sat down at its foot. She leaned back against the trunk. Her face was calm, but her eyes were wild as she watched and waited for what she was bringing upon herself.

After several moments, a long vine creeper wound its way up the trunk of the larch tree looping itself several times over a thick lower branch. Then it snaked its way down the trunk reaching the top of Jirri's head. Rennick watched as the vine slid over the Seraph's shoulder, coiling several times around her elegant neck before wrapping itself securely around the base of the tree. Jirri closed her eyes, and two infinitesimal tears rolled down her cheeks as she took a deep breath.

Then Rennick felt his sister instruct Jirri without saying a word. The female Seraph trembled in response, and the vine began tightening the coils around her neck, cutting deep into her flesh and closing off her airway. There was yet another sending from Jirri to the plant, a final command. Mercilessly, the vine snapped taut between the limb and the trunk, breaking Jirri's neck in a single, sickening crunch.

Rennick felt his eyes darken as he looked up at Raine, who stood gazing at Jirri's limp body with a look of grim satisfaction upon her face. Horrified, he was struggling to make sense of all that he had just witnessed.

Raine whispered, "The Balance is served."

The sound of cracking wood and falling debris snapped the twins' attention toward the skeleton of the still burning barn. They gasped in unison as they saw some of the fallen timbers moving, and ran back to investigate. Coming to a stop near what had once been the front of the barn, Raine and Rennick looked into the wreckage with wonder.

There, after pushing aside a large beam that had fallen over his broad shoulders, Kanias gathered himself off of the floor of the barn and

emerged slowly from a pile of smoldering rubble. He was covered in soot and his clothing was adorned with scorch marks and burn holes, but aside from a few superficial scratches, he appeared to be miraculously unscathed.

Brushing ash and dirt off of his body, Kanias began to move unsteadily through the debris toward the twins. Rennick reflexively moved to place himself between the Seraph and Raine, a reflection of that day's harsh lessons.

Kanias stopped when he noticed the movement, a pained look crossing his face. The burly man looked back toward what once was the barn's interior, where Jair's body lay impaled upon the enormous splinter of a support beam. Sighing, Kanias shook his head, and then looked toward Raine and Rennick with consoling, even apologetic eyes.

Rennick glanced unbidden toward Jair's broken body and recalled the words that had echoed in his head earlier.

Trust Kanias. He knows who you are.

"I tried to save him, to explain—," Kanias began, but upon meeting Raine's eyes, he stopped. The barrel-chested Seraph locked eyes with Rennick's sister. It appeared to be similar to the moment that she had earlier with Jirri, and Rennick could feel the tension rise within him as he expected the same confrontation.

Instead, Kanias' ash-covered face relaxed and his mouth broke into a thin, but genuine smile. He then bowed deeply toward each of the twins, reverently touching his forehead with both hands.

"Raine, you are the Realmwalker and Rennick is the Successor," Kanias said, his smile growing larger.

Raine nodded, and then looked at Rennick, who was too stunned to speak. Her eyes were a brighter shade of blue than they had ever been before and she wore confidence like a crown.

"I know," she said.

Chapter 10: Red

ONE look at the devastation that was the burning barn and the carnage in the clearing and Kanias was keenly aware of the situation that lay before him. The opaque smoke from the smoldering ruins swirling in the sky above gave him pause to consider what his next course of action should be.

It will not be long before someone from the village will come to investigate.

Tarien, Jirri and Jair were all dead, which was a problem. Kanias needed to devise a solution quickly.

The answer came to him.

“Raine and Rennick,” Kanias said. He staggered the rest of the way out of the wreckage, brushing away a few small embers clinging to his cloak. “We need to clean this up quickly,” he said, gesturing to Tarien and Jirri’s disfigured bodies. “Then leave before anyone comes to investigate. There will be plenty of time for questions later, I promise. But what we have to do will require both of you to place your trust with me.”

Kanias saw that Rennick was fighting with some emotion, and Raine now looked grim, but both seemed calm. They nodded simultaneously.

Good. They seem reasonably well, considering the ordeal.

"We need to move the bodies into the house," Kanias said, "And get your packs ready."

"Our packs are ready," Raine offered, a wash of what was most likely embarrassment appeared on her cheeks upon realizing what she had revealed. "Jair had us pack them when we arrived at the house."

So they were going to run.

Raine continued after a moment, her eyes growing darker. "I believe I know where Dani is," she said.

Rennick looked at his sister, his eyes hopeful and reserved at the same time. "Where is she," he said "Is she hurt?" Rennick's expression transitioned from concern to confusion "And why are you calling Mother and Father by their names?"

"Because they are not our real parents," Raine said articulately, with a compassionate look on her face. "Jirri murdered Dani. They were both Cou'Rali Adepts, in charge of raising us. Am I correct, Kanias?"

Dani? A Cou'Rali Adept? How did Raine find out all of this information?

Despite how unlikely it was to find a pair of Cou'Rali working together, Kanias somehow knew it to be true. He looked directly at Rennick. "I am afraid it is so," he said.

Rennick's shoulders slumped. Raine reached over and placed an arm around her brother's broad shoulders, tears rimming their eyes.

Kanias awkwardly shuffled his feet and turned to look back at the barn. He saw Jair's sword stuck into the ground near the place where he had moments before been buried beneath burning debris.

"Rennick, take your father's sword."

"But he was not my father." Rennick said slowly, eyes darkening. His demeanor was childlike and obstinate.

"Yes, he was." Raine said. "And Dani was our mother. They just were not our parents. I do not know how they ended up caring for us, but they did and they both died protecting us."

Rennick walked through the wreckage and up to the sword. He traced his fingers around the leather-wrapped hilt tied off by the sapphire. Rennick's eyes gradually grew lighter and he grasped the hilt and pulled the blade out of the ground.

"It feels strange," Rennick remarked as he inspected the hilt. "Heavy." The sword glinted in the afternoon sun, the sapphire a ball of blue fire catching Rennick's eye.

"Jair was left-handed," Kanias responded. "That is why it feels awkward in your grip. We can wrap for a right hand later. But now we have work to do."

"I think that I can find Dani," Raine said, "She should be just inside the thicket to the north of here."

"Go find her," Kanias said. "Then hurry back, and if you encounter anyone, please call for me." With that, Raine turned and ran across the lane toward the thicket.

Kanias turned to Rennick, who was still hypnotized by the sapphire at the end of Jair's sword. He placed a hand over the gemstone and captured Rennick's attention.

"You are a Seraph and also a Realmwalker," he said. "All of the Lani powers call to you, as do their gemstones. They desire your Bond with them, but you cannot allow the temptation to Bond with any gem to draw you in, because it is a lifetime bond, Yours is to be with the Sword of Angios one day."

Rennick's eyes widened and then lightened. He looked up at Kanias. "I do not understand what has happened today," he said.

"Neither do I." The Seraph raised his eyebrows and shook his head. "Not completely. But it is all true nonetheless." He looked up in time to see Raine disappear into trees near where he had stood earlier in the day to watch the farm. That had seemed like an entirely different time and place, not just this morning. "Now let us take care of the fallen," he said.

"We will care for my father first," Rennick said. He turned, sword in hand and began to wade through the debris to reach the fallen Cou'Rali. Kanias followed the Successor.

I wish I had learned the identity of their Master. It is apparent that Raine had discovered some information from Jirri and perhaps even Tarien. I will need to learn what she knows when the time is right.

They reached Jair, the body of the man Raine and Rennick knew as their father for eighteen years. They were able to pull him from the support beam without too much effort. Emotion punctuated Rennick's face as they raised Jair above the wreckage, the sword balanced upon the Maior's chest. No one spoke as they carried him across the lane, and then into the family's modest home. Upon entering, Rennick motioned with his head toward the rear of the house.

"We will lay him in their bed," Rennick said.

As they were placing Jair upon the bed, Kanias heard Raine at the door. He hurried to help her carry Dani into the house. He was surprised that she had moved the body so quickly and efficiently unaided. Together, they laid Dani to rest to the right of Jair on their bed, partners in death, just as they were in life.

Seeing the lifeless bodies of Jair and Dani underscored for Kanias the burden he now carried. Together, these two Adepts had managed to hide Raine and Rennick from the world for eighteen years, and yet, it all fell apart on them within a few hours. A small wave of panic washed over the Seraph as he pondered the implications of the day's events.

Two dead Cou'Rali. Two dead Seraph. The Realmwalker and the Successor found. An unknown Cou'Rali Master with questionable motives. And now it is up to me to lead them.

Kanias began to relax as he finally accepted the undeniable truth. He was alone. Until he knew more, or reached the Temple of Erta, he did not know anyone he could trust, even other Seraph. He had to get the twins to the Temple somehow, because that was where the Sword of Angios awaited the Realmwalker. However, if Jirri and Tarien's treachery was any indication, the Seraph of Natura were more fractured than Orrwyn, the leader of the Naturan Seraph and his mentor, believed them to be. That made the Temple a volatile and dangerous place for Raine and Rennick to go, but go there they must.

It is up to me.

Kanias looked up at the twins. Standing at the foot of the bed, they looked upon Jair and Dani with red rimmed eyes and blank expressions. Rennick's arm was draped over his sister's shoulder, his nearly jet black eyes glittering with bitter tears. Raine bowed her head and huddled closer to Rennick, one arm wrapped around her brother's waist. They supported one another.

They will need some time.

“You two stay here. I will prepare the others,” Kanias said.

They both nodded. “We will be out shortly.” Raine’s voice was sturdy yet soft.

Kanias was eager to leave the house, knowing that someone was sure to appear soon, wondering about the smoke.

I need more time.

The Seraph opened himself to D’ware, and time slowed. He ran over to where Jirri hung at the base of a larch tree. Her neck was pulled at a grotesque angle and her eyes were open, a dead light shining out from behind her dull gaze. Kanias shuddered.

Raine, wielding the grace and power of the Realmwalker, commanded Jirri to judge and sentence herself. I would not have believed it had I not felt it myself while I was under the rubble. Remarkable.

Carefully unwinding the vine from her neck, Kanias detached Jirri from the tree, lifting her over one shoulder. He moved swiftly toward the house, mindful of his surroundings. Upon entering, he placed Jirri in Raine’s bed and then returned to the place where Tarien had met his demise.

As Kanias approached the blood stained, turned up earth, his stomach churned. The sight of the ravaged Seraph was disturbing, as he had never seen a dead Seraph before. To see two within moments of each other was unheard of. It was not an experience that he cared to relive, but Kanias had a feeling that it was not going to be the last time. Raine had been found.

Tarien’s body was broken and trampled, making it that much more difficult to carry. As Kanias lifted it, he touched the grassy area with his Nym power, causing it to flourish and small white flowers to bloom. Under casual observation, it would appear that nothing unusual had happened there, but there was no hiding the blood soaked into the ground.

Kanias brought the Seraph’s corpse into the house and laid it in Rennick’s bed. He let go of D’ware, fighting the swirling world as he acclimated to the normal time stream again. He observed the table that was scattered with gear, which included two half-full travel packs. Kanias called for the twins.

Raine appeared first, followed by Rennick. He was still carrying the sword when they reached Kanias' side.

"Finish packing quickly, taking only what you need," he said. "We are burning the house. With any luck, they will assume that the bodies of Jirri and Tarien are you two, and no one will be the wiser."

The twins murmured their understanding and began grabbing random items from the table. Raine cinched up her pack, and after hoisting it upon her shoulders, returned to her room. Kanias recognized the familiar sound of a wooden drawer opening and closing. Shortly after, Raine returned, placing a small item in her belt pouch as she walked. By that time, Rennick was shouldering his own pack. Kanias didn't know what to do with the sword. Rennick did not have a scabbard and he not could simply walk around with bare steel glinting out in the open. To do so was asking for a fight. To leave it was out of the question. It was simply too valuable.

Another issue to be solved later.

Kanias surveyed the room and deduced that they had not left anything critical behind. He then turned on his heel and moved toward the door, Raine and Rennick close behind them. Once outside, he spied the small well with the bucket and winch at the side of the house. He walked over and looked down into the well. "Rennick, let me use the sword for a moment," he said.

Rennick handed Kanias the sword with which the Seraph cut the rope knot on the winch, and let the bucket and rope fall. After a couple of moments, they heard a small splash echo up from below.

"Why did you do that," Raine asked.

"We are lighting the house on fire," said Kanias. "But I do not want anyone able to be able stop the flames," replied Kanias. "We need to cover our tracks as much as possible, as we do not know who else might be coming, looking to do you two harm."

Kanias looked to the top of the house, the roof covered in rich green grass and a garden. "Rennick, please see if you can find a couple of pieces of burning timber from the barn." Rennick nodded and ran off. From where he was standing, Kanias could see several small flames still inhabiting a few of the thicker timbers, the same beams that had protected him from the falling walls earlier.

When he fell, Kanias was convinced that the barn would collapse on top of him, crushing him to death. If it failed to do that, it would certainly pin him down and burn him alive. But all he had was a cut on his forehead where a falling beam had hit him, causing him to lose consciousness briefly. When he awoke under the weight of the beams, he could feel the heat pressing in around him. Kanias could not believe his luck in landing in the one spot that would neither obliterate nor burn him alive. After all of that, including the wounds he suffered during his battle with Jair, he was remarkably uninjured.

Kanias inhaled deeply, turned, and looked at Raine. "How are you doing?" His question was simple, but he wanted her to answer with as many details as she felt comfortable providing.

"I am fine, thank you," she said. "But I am different."

Raine was taller than Kanias, so she had to tilt her head downward to look him in the eye. Kanias was honored by her gesture even though it was unintended. When he first pulled Raine out of the river, she did not carry herself as she did at that moment. The girl on the bank of the river was heroic and special to be sure. But the woman standing before him now was a paragon, one who would lead armies, and give hope to the masses.

"You are different," Kanias replied, feeling a small grin touch his lips. He did not want Raine to think that he was having any fun at her expense.

"Things are more vivid," she continued. "Clearer, but also more complex. Like the fact that Jair and Dani were not my parents. I have so many questions about it, like why I do not feel the same sort of sadness as Rennick. I know that I should, yet it makes sense that I do not."

Kanias nodded his head and continued with his assessment of Raine. She had been through a monumental transformation in the past few hours, yet she seemed so steady and sure of herself. This was not the same girl with eyes quick to tears. This was a woman of conviction, compassionate and empathetic, yet fierce and resilient. Built to survive. She was strong. Adaptable. Transcendent.

"That is normal," Kanias said, "When we first receive Spirit, we become more sensitive to certain types of emotions and stimulus. I would guess it is even more so for you and Rennick."

Raine turned her head to look at her brother as he picked his way through the rubble of the fallen barn.

"I worry about him," Raine said. "He feels what I feel, Kanias. He will not stop trying to protect me." Her eyes darkened slightly. "But who is going to protect him?"

Rennick approached them, carrying what appeared to be a singed brown sack as well as two arm-length pieces of barn siding still burning on one end.

"Look what I found," he said, holding the bag out in one hand for Kanias.

As Kanias reached for the bag, he realized that it was most likely the same bag he had seen at Jair's feet when he entered the barn earlier in the day. It occurred to him that its contents might require more than just a casual glance.

"Hold on to it Rennick. For now," Kanias said. "I want to take time to examine its contents, but now we need to hurry out of here."

Kanias took one piece of siding from Rennick and looked up at the grassy roof. Using Nym, he withered the grass, a wave of brown surging across the roof of the house. Then, using the siding as a brand, the Seraph ignited the freshly dying grass, sending plumes of gray and black smoke swirling into the air.

"I will return in a moment," Kanias said as he opened the door and entered the house for the last time. He closed and barred the door from the inside. In both bedrooms, he held the brand to the edges of all the bedding. When he finished, he placed it on top of the kindling pile sitting next to the small stack of firewood beside the hearth.

The all too familiar crackling sound of fire intensified as Kanias continued to ready the house. He picked up one of the chairs beside the table and flung it toward the large front window as he approached it. The chair shattered the glass, allowing him to jump through it. Once on the other side, he turned and scanned the area. Using Halen, he reached out to Cassie, who was contently eating grass far up the lane near the portage path. He asked her permission to see what she saw, and the cow granted it.

Kanias saw dark figures running up the road. That was all he needed. He thanked Cassie and cut off the connection. He looked at Raine and Rennick. "We need to go," he said. "Now."

Around the side of the house opposite the lane, Kanias moved into the trees. He was pleased to hear Raine and Rennick close behind him "As silently as possible, and no talking." His voice was hardly a whisper.

He led the twins south, away from the farm, traveling as quickly as possible with the trees as cover. They needed to return to the camp that Jirri had abandoned that morning. With the horses, water, and their gear still there, options for their trip to the Temple would be greater. When there failed to be any signs of active pursuit and Kanias determined that he and the twins were alone, he altered his course toward the east and spoke of his plan.

"We need the horses and gear," Kanias said. He spoke serenely as he looked into the darkening eyes of the twins. "Do you both know these woods well?"

The twins nodded in response.

The Seraph looked at Rennick first. "Can you lead us back to my camp quickly and without being seen?"

Rennick looked at Raine and then back to Kanias, perhaps wondering why the Seraph had not asked Raine to lead. "Of course," Rennick said.

Good. At least then, we might have a chance of escaping of Domo Vale unnoticed. And I can watch our backs.

Kanias was not worried about the local Neph. He had been in many villages where various individuals died due to Erta's judgment and he was never in any danger then. He was worried about other Seraph, however. Each of the three Seraph factions grew stronger daily, more entrenched and increasingly confident in what they considered to be the future for the Naturan Seraph. It was obvious that Jirri and Tarien were likely embedded in one of the more radical groups and were sent to kill him, Jair, Dani, the twins, or all of them for that matter. But until Kanias knew more information, he wanted to give the illusion that the assassinations had succeeded, especially in the eyes of those who wanted them dead, giving Kanias more time get the twins as far from Domo Vale as possible.

Rennick walked ahead several paces, leading them downward and then parallel to the small wrinkle in the hillside they were following.

He would cut his way through the trees to the east, and the others would follow. Raine seemed to know the way also, walking beside rather than behind Rennick, shadowing his winding course between the trees.

In the lower area, the trees were thicker, providing excellent cover. Kanias had worried that their travel would be louder and slower there than it would out be in the open. However, as he watched the twins effortlessly weave through the mass of tangled branches, he relaxed and concentrated on keeping up with them.

After about five minutes, Rennick stopped, as did Kanias and Raine seconds after. They crouched next to Rennick as he pointed to a break in the tree line where the portage path cut through the forest. Kanias nodded and crept closer to the trail, trying to get a clearer view of the area. Nothing appeared on the trail, and Kanias wished he felt secure enough to use his Lani abilities to help them scout ahead. It was an unfortunate trade-off, but now that they were on the run, not using the Lani was the best way to stay hidden.

Kanias turned and silently directed the twins to cross the path. Rennick looked up and down the path and then ran across it, continuing on into the foliage on the other side, with both Raine and Kanias following closely. Because the trees were further apart, Rennick increased his speed bringing them closer to their goal.

A few moments later, they came over a small rise where the river and the camp were at last visible amid the trees below them. The horses, aware of their presence, picked up their heads and whinnied. Kanias quickly perused the camp, concluding that it looked as it had a few hours earlier. The Seraph's packs were still intact and the horses appeared to be undisturbed. It was unlikely that anyone had been at the camp since Jirri had left it, but he could not be sure.

"We are here," Kanias said quietly, "But I am not convinced we are safe yet."

These words sounded strange coming from Kanias. Being a Seraph, he was seldom worried about being seen, much less hunted, especially when he traveled in the Neph settlements. In fact, beings everywhere went out of their way not to even look in the direction of a Seraph.

Of course! We are all Seraph. Three traveling together.

Kanias made his way over to the pile of packs and bags at the foot of a brown, quick-footed mare. "Raine," said Kanias, "Please find Jirri's armor and any other clothing of hers and see if it fits you."

Raine was a few inches taller than Jirri, but they had a similar physique. While the leggings and boots would be out of the question, everything else would fit well enough to be functional.

Kanias motioned for Rennick to do the same with the gear beside the tall roan stallion that was Tarien's. He then walked over to his own horse, Majan.

The mare whinnied tenderly as she saw her master approach. Reaching up, Kanias held the gray horse's head and patted her muzzle. While she was not as tall as Tarien's horse, and not as fast as Jirri's, Majan was sure-footed and strong. They had been traveling companions for years, and Kanias was certain that she was confused due to his lack of mental greeting.

"Lovely girl," Kanias purred under his breath, giving the animal reassuring pats on the neck and shoulders.

Kneeling over his items at the base of Majan's tree, Kanias located his own close-fitting, hard leather armor. Removing one of the two broaches emblazoned with the yelta that cinched his cloak, Kanias was able to slide into the side of the armor. Setting it squarely upon his shoulders, he buckled the straps tightly to himself before pulling the cloak tightly around his neck again, securing it with the broach. He then picked up a pair of thick, hard leather bracers also emblazoned with the yelta, and buckled them onto his lower arms.

Kanias looked up to check on the twin's progress and saw that Rennick was following his lead, attempting to put on Tarien's armor. But Raine was motionless beside Jirri's pile, studying something she was holding in her hands. Curious, he stood and walked over to see what she had found.

Looking up with dark eyes as Kanias approached, Raine's face was tight with emotion. Not saying a word, Raine held out a scrap of paper. Kanias took it, his curiosity turning to apprehension.

Rennick wandered to Kanias' side, the armor clumsily hanging on only one of his shoulders. It was a corner of paper, with torn edges on two sides and as wide as his palm. In the middle, in red ink and penned in an even hand, there was one word.

RED.

"What is that supposed to mean?" Rennick said.

"Where did you find this?" Kanias said. The gray pallor of dread blushed over his face.

"It was in her pack," Raine replied, staring fixedly at the scrap of paper in his hands. "Whatever it means, I am certain that word on this scrap of paper and what transpired today at the farm are connected." She then locked eyes the Seraph. "What do you know about this?'

Kanias knew that Raine was correct. Too much had happened that particular day for there to be any coincidences. To find this in Jirri's belongings and have it not relate to the events was very unlikely. Unfortunately, Kanias had no idea what it meant, who wrote it, or what to do about it for that matter. He was unprepared to offer any answers and it was not an opportune time to discuss the reasons why.

"I agree that it probably has something to do with all that has occurred today," Kanias said. "And that the bag Rennick found may contain clues, but we will have to investigate these later. Now, we need to get as far away from here as possible."

The Seraph turned toward Rennick who was still working to tighten the straps properly on Tarien's armor. Kanias helped him with the myriad of belts and buckles used to ensure a proper fit. "First, you will both need to wear the armor and the yelta broaches to hold your cloaks in place," Kanias said. He had to loosen the shoulder straps of Tarien's armor to fit Rennick. Tarien was tall and strong, but Rennick was broader through the back and chest.

"And both of you will need to accompany me to the Temple," Kanias continued. "Part of my plan to get you there in one piece is to dress you as Seraph do when they travel. Our journey may be under surveillance and we cannot hope to avoid meeting other travelers along the way."

Rennick flexed and then flinched as Kanias tightened the last strap. Bending down, he grabbed Tarien's bracers and handed them to Rennick, who took them and began strapping them onto his arms.

Kanias felt a thread of D'ware in use behind him. He spun around only to see Raine standing with the armor balanced properly on her shoulders, her hands a blur of action as she worked and reworked the straps. Kanias watched in mix of interest and surprise as the armor molded itself around her torso, as if it were a malleable object. One last flurry of Raine's hands, and the armor looked as if she had worn it forever, that it was custom made for her and perfectly fitted to her body. The smile that flashed across Raine's face morphed into a look of surprise as she stumbled slightly, catching her balance with trunk of the tree beside her. Kanias' nervous eyes flickered around the trees as a precautionary measure, suppressing a smile in the process.

"When you manipulate time, the shift of stopping too abruptly will make you dizzy." Kanias' tone was cautionary but encouraging. "The longer you use it, and the slower or faster that you go, the stronger the effect will be. Moreover, the more attention you will have to pay when coming out of it." Kanias looked at Raine to address her directly.

"That was an amazing use of the power, Raine," he said. "But you need to remember that any Seraph could have felt your Lani for miles in every direction, especially in an area like this where there are no other Lani users."

Raine's eyes darkened a shade as she spoke. "I was only trying to be efficient and save time," she said. "I figured that learning how to put on the armor quickly could save my life."

Rennick shuffled nervously beside Kanias. But it was Kanias' turn to be embarrassed.

Here I am, worried about a possible threats, and I am chastising the Realmwalker for wanting to protect her own life in the best way possible, in the way she sees fit.

"I apologize, Raine," Kanias said, bowing and touching his head. "Let us hurry out of this area, so we can put our minds at ease. As you two pack and become acquainted with your horses, I will pack the camp and ready my own horse."

The camp was easy to break down, for Jirri had completed any of the tasks for setting up the camp that Kanias had assigned her earlier. Aside from the cooking tripod, kettle, and cups, there was not much for him to collect. As Kanias gathered the items from around the campfire, he took a moment to rake the dirt and rocks that Tarien had excavated back over the remaining fire. In an attempt to camouflage the disturbed earth, he scattered dead leaves and twigs over the area. It was not much, and would not hold up to scrutiny, but without using Nym, it was the best he could manage.

It will have to do. The illusion is that Raine and Rennick are dead. Not that we were never here at all.

As Kanias walked back to Majan, he could see that both Raine and Rennick were nearly finished saddling their horses. The saddles were designed for travel, so attaching the assortment of gear to various buckles and hangers was easy, albeit time consuming. The trick was to cinch the leather straps tightly to prevent anything shifting while the horse was moving.

Within a few moments, they were all packed. The twins mounted their packs on top of the bedrolls tied behind the saddles. The packs were bulky, but until they could take the time to determine which items were essential and which were not, they needed to take all of it. Rennick had strapped Jair's sword to the top of his pack. The blade was covered, but the hilt still jutted out on one side, the sapphire sparkling in the afternoon light. Kanias realized that the sword would always draw attention, even more so if it were stowed properly in a scabbard at Rennick's side.

But it is his sword now. I just have to be certain he knows how to use it before he wears it.

The last things that Kanias took were the three metal-clad quarterstaves leaning against the tree. Using the strap made for that purpose, he affixed them diagonally to his back, the left side up, allowing him to safely mount and ride his horse.

He turned to see that Raine and Rennick had mounted their horses. Raine was guiding the brown mare in a weaving pattern through some nearby trees, speaking to her softly under her breath. The finely muscled brown mare moved easily under Raine's guidance. By contrast, Rennick was holding the reins awkwardly in his outstretched hands, and appeared to be at odds with his horse. The light-sided horse fidgeting beneath him, sensing Rennick's anxiety and nervousness, was irritable if not obstinate.

"Relax, Ren." Raine called out to him. "The horse can feel you. If you are calm, your horse will be calm as well."

Kanias rode up alongside Rennick, taking advantage of the

opportunity to use a touch of Halen to soothe the animal. A friendly nicker from Rennick's horse indicated a noticeable change its disposition showing Kanias that all was well and that he could let go of the Lani.

"We are headed to the hills above Domo Lake tonight," Kanias said looking at each of them. "While we travel, you will not use your real names, or call attention to yourselves in any way. Until we reach the Temple, Raine receives the Sword, and you both are trained, you both are potentially vulnerable." He heeled Majan forward so he could speak more discreetly.

"If we are in danger, we may be under watch," Kanias said. "And every movement we make may be noted." Kanias took each of them by the eye. Rennick looked determined, but his eyes shifted rapidly from side to side, as if he expected to see shadowy figures lurking from behind the surrounding trees. Raine smiled bravely and nodded.

"We need anyone watching to believe that three Seraph entered Domo Vale, and that three left Domo Vale with a Neph family dead upon their departure," Kanias said. "It may be unusual but not impossible. Seraph are rarely questioned. If we are lucky, no one will know or suspect anything different. But I need you both to assume the role of Seraph. For now Rennick, you are Tarien. You, Raine, are Jirri."

A slight look of disdain crossed Raine's face at the mention of the names, but she and her brother nodded in agreement.

Kanias continued. "I am known in some of these areas, so please allow me to speak for all of us if we encounter anyone. And remember, we are being truthful. You are both Seraph."

The last bit had the intended effect on the twins. Raine's posture improved in the saddle, and the emblems on her chest seemed to catch a few more beams of the late afternoon sun. Rennick smiled and he squared his shoulders. Their eyes lightened several of shades, and were wide and clear. They were Seraph, and they were ready.

Chapter 11: First Night

THEY traveled as close to the riverbank as possible, moving upriver toward Domo Lake. Kanias instructed the twins to stay close and to remain confident. It was apparent that Kanias was concerned about meeting other individuals along the way, perhaps even other Seraph. But after what happened at the farm, Rennick was not sure if the Seraph's concern was for their safety alone. The trouble was that Raine did not know the limits of her own power.

She is The Realmwalker. What does that make me? Just a Seraph? What does it mean to be the Successor, other than to take over if Raine dies?

Rennick glanced in the direction of his sister. He felt a change in both of them when she transformed during her encounter with Jirri. He felt stronger and faster, but he did not feel like Raine looked. Aside from her long hair, Raine looked in every way a Seraph. From how she held herself to the way she seemed to exude both mystery and power, no one looking at Raine would ever doubt that she was one of Erta's Chosen. Compared to her, however, Rennick felt clumsy and awkward. Until that point, he always felt as though he and his sister were fairly equal. There was no equality now, however. Rennick did not have to test her to know that it was not even close.

Take care of Raine!

The words from Jair echoed in Rennick's mind once again. It was nearly impossible for him to comprehend that the man he knew as his father was not. He wanted to know the truth. To ask questions and have the answers that satisfied him. His head was spinning from all of the changes and he merely wanted something to make sense in his life again.

They made good time as the trees were thick enough to provide some cover from those traveling on the portage path, yet sparse enough nearer to the bank so they could ride quickly. The horses' hooves sprung lightly over the soft, mossy turf. Several times, Kanias would stop them when he heard the sound of a wagon or another rider on the path to their right. Travelers were always coming from the lake and heading downstream toward Domo Vale.

After an hour, the trees thinned, allowing them to see a hundred strides ahead. They finally reached the point where the portage path cut in tightly against the river along the shore of the lake; they could not avoid it anymore. It was then that Kanias slowed, and then stopped his gray mare, turning to speak to Raine and Rennick.

"We now have to make a choice," the Seraph said before looking through the trees at the lake ahead. "We can either make for the ford that crosses the Pyn ahead or we can curve around the south side of the lake and travel in the hills up to Jaske Green." Kanias said, gesturing toward the southeast.

Raine looked to both directions, listening to Kanias' every word.

"The ford is shorter, but is more open and heavily used," she offered. "The way south is more concealed, but much longer and more tedious."

Rennick nodded in agreement, and Kanias eyed each of them from head to toe, weighing them with his stare. He made a decision

"We will take the ford," he said. "From this point forward, you both are the Seraph initiates, Tarien and Jirri, and you're on your first training assignment with me. Please, do not speak unless spoken to. Do not look anyone in the eye. And do not, under any circumstances, use your abilities unless it is in self-preservation. We do not want to call more attention to ourselves than we already do."

Rennick met his sister's gaze, and while he still sensed feelings of lingering sadness inside of her, she projected poise and authority. Rennick tried to emulate his sister's posture, but he felt silly. Only when he caught glimpses of the yelta on his shoulders and arms did he relax. No one ever doubted that symbol of power.

Several moments passed until they met the lane alongside the river where Kanias directed them to pick up the pace. The riverbank gradually sloped toward the water, the far side growing steadily steeper with each stride their horses took. The trees became shorter and more scattered. They were riding in the open now, so it was no surprise that Rennick could see several groups of individuals ahead conducting business on the docks, the small portage buildings, and the ford used to cross the Pyn.

The portage path continued to widen until it became a road, paved with large irregular sheets of flat gray rock. The horses' hooves clacked as they walked, but as far as Rennick can tell, no one appeared to take more than a casual notice of their passing.

Neph. I used to be one of them.

The docks were busy that day, as it was Yelta Luna. This meant local provisions were arriving from the surrounding areas, all in anticipation of markets eager to provide customers with goods to fill their empty shelves after the Carna Lunas celebrations had ended.

Horses and wagons lined the docks where several Neph were lifting wooden crates out of boats and carrying them to waiting wagons. There were Neph families in the area that made their money working as porters, bringing goods down the portage trail and then loading them onto various boats in Domo Vale destined for elsewhere. No boats were allowed past the ford, however, as the water was made shallow by the addition of the large, flat-topped rocks, making it all but impossible for a boat to float over it. Without that obstacle, it was likely that some traders would prefer to risk the rapids rather than pay the portage fees.

The road turned toward the water, and then curved toward the shoreline. The late afternoon sun light played on the surface of swirling eddies of the dark river. The water was only a few inches deep at the ford, but it was swift, requiring them to slow the horses' pace so they could walk safely and without hesitation. After a few moments, Kanias had his horse climbing out onto the landing on the other side. Raine and Rennick followed Kanias, who turned to watch the twins on the off chance that one of their horses slipped. However, his eyes were drawn upward where they locked onto a fixed point in the sky. His shock was evident.

Raine and Rennick rode out of the water and turned in their saddles to see what Kanias was looking at. In the distance to the northwest, a large cloud of the blackest smoke they had ever seen rose above the tree line. It was hovering above Domo Vale. The late afternoon sun tinged the cloud with pearly hues of orange and red. Rennick could see Neph on each side of the river shading their eyes to look at the sky, watching the large cloud with apprehension.

"By the Goddess," Rennick murmured.

Raine stood in her stirrups and turned her gaze down the river as if she were ready to ride across it and return to her home immediately. Rennick could feel his sister's instinctive desire to help those in need, and he could feel the pull himself as well.

"You both stay close." Kanias' voice was sharp, edged with concern. "We are leaving."

Raine gave Kanias a puzzled look. She wanted to say something, but instead she stared at him flatly as she passed him slowly on her horse. Rennick sensed his sister's frustration and anger roll off her as rain rolls off a pitched roof. Raine knew tragedy had struck Domo Vale and she wanted to help. The urge was as powerful as her need to breathe.

She rode up the landing, stiff in the saddle as she turned her back upon the only life she had ever known. Kanias watched as Rennick too rode by him looking defeated. The Seraph hurried his horse to fall in beside the Successor.

"I am sorry Rennick," Kanias said. "I really am."

Rennick knew that Kanias was sincere, but his main concern was Raine. "Say it to her," Rennick said quietly, nodding toward Raine.

Kanias nodded in agreement. "She is going to need you to be

strong for her," he said. "What I say Rennick, does not matter."

Kanias clucked at his gray mare and moved up to Raine, who was about twenty feet in front of her brother. His bald head gleaming in the heat of the sun, he leaned over to whisper something in her ear. Raine's posture relaxed slightly and she turned to look at Kanias directly. She nodded. It appeared that they had reached some sort of agreement.

"Keep up," Kanias called back to Rennick, "We need be at the bluffs before it gets too dark."

Rennick urged the roan faster, but Kanias and Raine had already reached the end of the paved road where it turned into a dirt trail. Kanias whispered to Majan, and the horse took off in a streak of gray. Raine was not far behind. It was then that Rennick leaned into the neck of his horse, feeling the heat of its body transfer into his own limbs. A bolt of energy shot through them both and they bounded faster, following in cloud of dust Kanias and Raine left behind.

The bluffs from the Domo Hills rose hard against the northern shoreline of both Domo Lake and the Pyn River, requiring them to skirt the shoreline of the lake in order to climb the first set of trails leading up and over the bluffs that awaited them. The shoreline was flat, punctuated with an array of short trees and shrubs. A narrow path snaked its way over the face of the bluffs, weaving between the soft, swampy areas and the occasional willow that grew right up to the water's edge. The existence of the bluffs was the very reason for traffic to use the lake and the river to reach the surrounding area.

The path and its soft, loamy soil provided the perfect surface for the horses to run. The roan was faster than the others, and longed to be in a race to prove the point. But the path was narrow, and therefore not safe.

Kanias was in front, and Rennick could see that he was scouting to the left, looking for something at the base of the nearby bluffs. At last, he spotted what he was searching. As a result, he slowed his horse to a trot, and turned to the left, and exited the trail. Raine and Rennick were close behind, and Rennick could see that they were moving toward a thick line of trees swaying back and forth across the face of the nearest bluff.

"This is our way up," Kanias called back to them.

As they approached the base of the bluff, Rennick realized that the line of trees was sheltering a narrow path of crushed rock. It cut severely into the steep slope of the bluff. Slowing Majan to a walk as they neared the trail, Kanias turned to speak with them both.

"We will stop for the night at the top of this bluff," he said. He gestured toward the bluff, his eyes squinting in the sunlight. "It should provide shelter enough for the night, as well as a better view of the area at dawn."

Kanias urged Majan up the abrupt incline that was the path, Raine and Rennick following closely. They walked along the path for about three hundred strides when it cut deep into the side of the bluff, then turned back and wound its way up the face of the bluff again. Facing northwest, rising high above the tree line, they were able to see clearly for miles despite the diminishing light of day.

The lake was so clear that it appeared bottomless, so blue that it matched the sky. The river, like a silk ribbon, curved toward the blaze of the orange sun. Black bands of smoke hung heavily over the forest, playing off what remained of the light behind them. Rennick could see several lines of Neph exiting the trees, coming from the direction of Domo Vale. The clearing leading toward the dock and portage area looked as though someone kicked over an ant hill. Those leaving Domo Vale mixed with those who were working and waiting at the docks, thus inciting confusion. Panic had taken hold below.

The trail turned again, mercifully so since it drew the trio's attention away from the drama unfolding below them. But the respite was short-lived as they were given a full view of the Pyn valley each time the trail doubled back to the north. There too, Rennick could sense the sadness and pain that Raine felt. It was the feeling that she was abandoning those she could readily help in their time of need.

Kanias carefully studied the area below as they continued to ride, looking for anyone who may have forded the river to head into the bluffs. It was clear, however, that the Neph were intent on sticking together.

As the sun continued to drop toward the horizon, they reached the top of the bluff. Rennick had waited until that point to venture a question.

"Kanias," he said. "What do you think happened?"

Kanias shook his head. "I do not know, but I am certain about one thing. The fire at the farm was not the cause. And until we have more information, we need to be very cautious of supposing anything without all the facts."

They turned right, following the path along the ridge for a few strides until it angled to the left. The path sloped down the hill for about a hundred feet before a narrow trail split off from it, running a few strides before spilling into a small grove of trees. Its final location would not only conceal them from other travelers on the path to and from valley below, but it was also close to water. There was a spring nearby, one that sent a continuous rivulet of water flowing down the eastern side of the bluff.

Kanias dismounted his horse in the center of the small sylvan alcove. "This will do for now," the Seraph said, investigating the area before beginning to unpack Majan.

"Is this a safe place for us to stop," Raine asked.

"There is no such thing as safe for you two anymore," Kanias replied. "We will have to take watch while we rest. The sun is only down here for about an hour before it starts rising again. So that is when I will take my shift."

Rennick was struck by the manner-of-fact way that Kanias admitted that they were not safe anywhere. The twins looked at one another. Rennick could not only see, but feel the weight of everything press down upon Raine. In fact, it was all beginning to crush her.

"How are you," he asked.

"I am failing already," she said. "I do not know what I am doing, or why I am doing it. Everything has changed, and I feel myself losing my grip. So many people, Rennick. I could feel their suffering." Raine's exhausted body folded in on itself and fell to the ground. Quivering, she pulled her knees inward. Her breathing was rapid and each of her eyes was a small glassy black abyss.

Kanias was at her side in an instant. "Breathe, Raine. Everything is going to be okay," he said. But even he did not sound convinced by his own words.

After several awkward moments, Raine sat up straight and wiped the tears from her cheeks. Then she stood. "I am the Realmwalker, protector and defender." Her voice thick with emotion, dripping with sarcasm.

"Nonsense," Kanias said, smiling. "The most important quality that a Realmwalker can possess is empathy. That is how they balance their own power, by remaining compassionate. But also by exercising restraint." Kanias looked up at Rennick and nodded at him, as if to reassure him that Raine would be fine if she would just calm herself.

"Gather some wood," he said. "It's time to build a fire."

Rennick heeded Kanias' direction and began scavenging the dead wood that lay scattered beneath the trees. There was plenty to be found, and he had a large armful in just a few moments. With little forethought, Rennick began assembling them into a small pile near where Raine now sat, Kanias watching over her and evaluating his fire building capabilities.

When Rennick finished the wood pile, Kanias produced from his saddlebag a small waxed paper package. Unfolding the wax paper carefully in the fading light, he revealed several short sticks tipped in a hard white substance.

"These are firebrands," he said. "From Elementa. Watch carefully."

Holding a firebrand, Kanias pressed his thumbnail against the tip and flicked it quickly. To Rennick's amazement, a small, but vigorous flame erupted from the white material encasing the tip of the firebrand. The process emitted a small curl of acrid smoke that momentarily stung his nostrils. The tiny flame settled into a hot tongue of fire on the end of the stick, the white material completely consumed. Casually holding it to the dry leaves and kindling pile that Rennick had built, Kanias lit the fire. Within seconds, it was burning bright and warm.

"We will not make a full camp tonight," he said as returned to his horse. "We will unburden the horses, but leave everything packed. I want to be able to leave quickly, if necessary."

Rennick worked swiftly to remove the saddles and gear from the backs of both his and Raine's horses, setting the items at the foot the same tree to which each horse was tied. He pulled Raine's and his own bedroll out of their bindings and walked over to the fire. Kanias was busy sifting through some other small wrapped packages, already having assembled the cooking tripod and setting it over the fire. A kettle was brewing the tea Rennick remembered so well from earlier that morning. It flavored the chilly evening air with its refreshing spicy tang.

Raine was again sitting with her knees pulled up to her chest. Dropping to her side, Rennick placed their bedrolls behind them, and then looked at his sister. He knew she was still disheartened, but could sense that some of the pressure had been lifted from her.

Rennick looked at his sister. Before the question parted his lips, she answered him.

"I just became overwhelmed, that's all" Raine said. "I am so tired."

Kanias reached around the fire, handing each of them a small package of dried meat and cheese. They both ate quickly and quietly. Rennick had not realized how hungry he had been until he saw the food sitting in his hand. He and Raine were still picking at the small crumbs littering the paper when he heard Kanias chuckle.

"I know it was not much," he said. "We need to ration our food until we get to Jaske Green. However, I do have these." Kanias revealed a small burlap sack and a wide smile.

It was Raine and Rennick's turn to laugh. At last, they could finally eat their maoli.

Chapter 12: The Road to Jaske Green

THE chirping of birds woke Rennick the next morning. He bolted upright, startled to find that he was not at home in Domo Vale amid the heaps of blankets that covered his goose down bed. The realization shook him from the last vestiges of his dreamless sleep until he was finally able to focus on the details of the small but efficient camp that he, Kanias, and Raine had made the night before.

It took Rennick a moment to locate the others through the thin veil of fog draped over them. They were sitting at the top of the bluff, above the camp, looking to the west toward Domo Vale. They spoke to each other in low voices so not to wake Rennick. Seeing their silhouettes reminded Rennick of his rock at home, how he would spend hours day dreaming about the world beyond Domo Vale, about a life where he would not have to answer to his parents.

His parents.

A sickness settled at the base of Rennick's gut. The fact was that Jair and Dani Sherrill were not the parents of his birth, but his parents nonetheless. That they were dead seemed impossible. There was no question that they loved Rennick, and that they loved Raine. And there was no question as to their devotion, whether blood was more powerful than the heart. It was not, for blood is accountable to the heart every time. But there were other questions, such as the twins' true identity and why they were raised by those who were not their parents. But he had to put it behind him for the moment. If he did not, it would consume him and there was too much at stake.

Stretching his arms above his head and arching his back, it occurred to Rennick that he had fallen asleep without removing his leather armor, or even unfolding his bedroll, using it instead as a pillow. The muscles of his legs and abdomen were tight, sore from the prior day's wide array of activity that ranged from nearly drowning to watching his childhood home burn to the ground. His ribs burned with each breath, the aching surely compounded by sleeping on the hard ground. Wearing the armor held them intact, however. Encased in the armor as if it were a shell, it supported his bruised frame so that he felt little pain when he was upright.

Climbing the path to the top of bluff, Rennick massaged his legs into compliance, knowing that they would be called into action again shortly. Kanias and Raine both looked down when they heard him. Raine looked tired, but her eyes were brighter, and there was an aura of understanding and acceptance surrounding her.

She is feeling better, feeling something other than remorse.

Kanias stood as Rennick approached. "How are you?" Rennick suspected that Kanias knew the answer.

"I feel like I swam all morning, ran all afternoon, and rode a horse until nightfall," said Rennick. He couldn't help but to smile, but worried that the Seraph would take offense. He was relieved when instead Kanias let loose a hardy chuckle.

"I said the same thing to him earlier," Raine said, standing to walk over to them, also appearing to be stiff and sore.

Rennick's smile grew. He looked eastward to where the sun was rising over the green tops of the Domo Hills. "Why did you let me sleep so long" he said to Kanias. "I thought that we were leaving at first light?"

"Both you and Raine require as much as time to recover as possible after yesterday," Kanias replied. "We have a long way to travel, and I want you both to be as rested as time will allow."

"What about the trouble in Domo Vale?" Rennick was suddenly

aware of the severity of the situation and it renewed his concern. "Isn't someone looking for us?"

"After both of you fell asleep, I took a chance and reached out with my Lani to gather some information." Kanias began to walk down to the camp, beckoning the twins to follow. "I was able to determine that we are not being followed, at least not yet. But I also felt a continual stream of troubling information. Plant, animal, and being all had the same energy flowing through them, both restless and suspicious. Something just does not make any sense."

"What," Rennick asked as he retrieved his bedroll so he could pack it with the rest of his gear on it the roan stallion.

"Three beings walking through Domo Vale, lighting everything on fire," Kanias said. The twins noticed a hint of hesitancy in the Seraph's voice that he was deliberately trying to mask. "At first, I thought that perhaps I misunderstood the information being relayed to me," he continued. "But I now know it is something else. Something so horrible that to even speak of it frightens me."

The twins were stunned. The mighty Seraph Kanias just said that to speak of something frightened him. It was fear, not concern or even worry that illustrated the Seraph's face. Rennick could feel additional anxiety pulse from Raine, as if her entire body were throbbing from the pressure of what burdened her. Kanias' news made matters worse. In a day of such tragic events, however extraordinary, what Kanias said next seemed too bizarre to believe.

"Unknown to everything that grows, crawls, or walks in this Realm, it was something none has ever seen before, but exists all the same," he said. "It is a being that hurls balls of fire that water cannot extinguish."

Rennick imagined such beings walking through the village, lighting the places he remembered from his youth on fire. It seemed as though everything in his past was destined to burn.

Whatever it was, it was in Domo Vale because of us. And it is out there still.

Kanias offered Rennick another package of dried meat and cheese, along with a cup of tea from the kettle still sitting on the tripod over the smoldering coals. "Eat now, and prepare. Raine and I will ready the horses."

Rennick sat and watched in silence as his sister and Kanias packed and loaded the horses for travel. As the Seraph arranged Rennick's gear, he stopped and pulled out the burlap bag that Rennick had discovered under a partially burned beam in the middle of what had been his family's barn. Walking toward him, Kanias opened the bag, and pulled out two different items. The first was a small leather pouch, and the second was a soft leather scabbard. Opening the pouch, Kanias looked inside to inspect the contents.

"Raine, come here a moment, please." Kanias called over to her without looking up. Raine finished securing something to the left side of her saddle and then joined them beside the fire.

"What we have here is very interesting," he said. Kanias referred to the burlap sack in his hand, "I saw this bag at Jair's feet when he was inside the barn."

Rennick saw Raine's face cloud momentarily. It was apparent that she was overpowered by a memory. He could feel his own mood, and subsequently his eyes, subtly darken.

"Put your hand out, Raine," Kanias said, offering the open pouch.

Raine extended her hand in which Kanias poured the pouch's contents. The coins clinked softly, one after the other until a large green gem dropped into their center with a thud. Raine let out a slow breath, and her eyes brightened to light blue.

Rennick felt himself leaning over in awe to look at the handful of gold and green in his sister's hand. It was easily more wealth than either he or his sister had ever seen before. Rennick had seen a gold coin once during Yelta Luna, when a traveling Neph vendor had shown it off to the local villagers as proof of the quality of his products. He said the gold coin was paid to him in the markets of Gran Dak. That day, every young Neph's mind, including Rennick's was set ablaze with dreams of leaving Domo Vale in search of adventure only to return home to a hero's welcome, bags of gold in tow. That was the power of *one* gold piece. Rennick was staring at over a dozen.

Then there was the gem. Immeasurably green, it was one of the most beautiful things that Rennick had ever seen. The Emerald's Glow in Domo Vale had a real emerald embedded into the mosaic over the mantle of the fireplace inside the main tavern hall. This particular gem was not only five times as large, and twice as dark, but it was so deeply green that it appeared to have a green flame dancing in its center.

Its glimmer called to Rennick to the point that he reached out to touch it. A gentle, but firm hand grasped his wrist. It was that of Kanias.

"I'm sorry Rennick," Kanias said with a hint of concern. "But you are going to be susceptible to the desire to Bond with any gem that you come into contact with. That is until we get Raine to the Sword of Angios."

Rennick gave the Seraph a questioning look. It was obvious that he did not understand.

"I will explain as we travel," Kanias said. "I know that this emerald was Dani's, just as the sapphire in the sword was Jair's. But I do not know what all this was for," he said sifting a handful of the coins through his fingers. "Or what your father was doing with it."

Kanias took what remained in Raine's hand from her and funneled it back into the pouch. Then he opened the burlap, reached in, and pulled out the leather scabbard.

"I suspect that this is for Jair's sword," Kanias said. "Let us see." Kanias walked over to Rennick's gear and retrieved the sword that was sitting on top of his travel pack. He carefully slid the sword into the scabbard until it stopped against the hilt with a thud.

"It fits," he said. "And for now, it stays here." Kanias placed the sword on top of the pack again, looking deliberately in Rennick's direction.

He then jingled the pouch. "This is your money," he said to the twins. "I am simply holding it for you as we travel because as a Seraph of a certain standing, it would not be unusual for me to have gold coins and a jewel. It might raise eyebrows, however, if two unshaven Seraph initiates were in possession of such luxuries."

Kanias tied the pouch to his belt, and turned back to load Rennick's horse. Raine shrugged her shoulders and walked toward her own horse to finish readying it for travel.

"I could wear the sword," Rennick said with a hopeful intonation. He stuffed the last of the cheese Kanias gave him into his mouth all at once, seeing Raine wrinkle up her nose in disgust. She then looked to see

Kanias' reaction.

Rennick stammered as he continued, speaking with his mouth full. "It might be useful, that is. If we run into a dangerous situation, wouldn't it be better for me to have a sword handy and at the ready, than tied down to the back of the horse?"

Without hesitation, Kanias untied the bundle that held the sword to Rennick's pack. He pulled the gleaming blade from the scabbard. Walking over to him, Kanias offered the sword hilt to Rennick, and leaned the scabbard against a nearby tree.

"Stand up and take your weapon, Rennick," the Seraph said with a steady voice.

Rennick stuffed the last piece of meat into his mouth, wiped his hands against his leggings as he stood, and reached for the hilt with his right hand. The leather wrapping did not conform particularly well to his hand, but he could still grip it.

The weight of the sword was perfectly balanced, and it seemed easy to hold and maneuver the blade. Rennick could feel the cool presence of the sapphire against his wrist, and imagined it was whispering to him.

Kanias smiled. "Ready your sword, Successor," he said to Rennick sweeping his cloak behind both shoulders.

Rennick could feel Raine behind him radiating both interest and skepticism. She laughed as she called out to Rennick. "Get him, Ren," although she was not particularly convincing.

Rennick flung his cloak back in the same fashion as did Kanias, and took several practice swings. He then held out the sword before him. "Read—"

Kanias was a blur. Before Rennick realized it, the Seraph had bent time and the next thing he knew, he was flung onto his back. The air in Rennick's lungs escaped in a rush. The leather absorbed some of the shock, but his sore ribs wrenched and pain shot through them. The sword was in Kanias' left hand, the point tapping Rennick under the chin. Raine giggled.

"You just died by your own sword," Kanias said. His voice was serious, but instructive. "Remember, you gave an enemy a powerful weapon to use against others. A weapon to use against me. Against Raine!"

Kanias quickly pulled the weapon away from Rennick's chin with a jerk, then outstretched his hand to Rennick, who accepted it so that he could stand. Rennick dusted himself off, Kanias brushing more dirt away as he clapped him on the back.

"*This* is your weapon," Kanias said, lightly tapping Rennick's head with his finger. He then took the scabbard and slowly walked back to the roan stallion to return it to where it had been. "But any weapon is useless," he continued. "Until you know how to use it."

"I understand, Kanias," Rennick replied as he walked up to his horse.

"Do not worry," Kanias said. "Before we are done with your training at the Temple, you will not only know the art of the sword, but you will also be able to utilize your Lani abilities appropriately and understand the ways of Cou'Rali as well." Kanias turned to his saddle and belongings to pack his horse.

Raine walked to her brother's side "Don't worry," she said. "We will learn together, and we will get better. You will see." She smiled at him, the same smile she employed whenever she wanted to make him feel better, especially in the case of soothing his ego. Rennick could feel his sister's confidence and self-assurance. He wished that he felt the same. But from the moment he was on his back, seeing Jair's sword in the Seraph's hand, he realized how ill prepared he truly was to face this strange new reality. He looked over to his sister as she checked the ties on the last few items attached to her saddle.

How am I going to protect her if I am not ready? I will get better, but I will not wait until we arrive at the Temple. I must know more.

After they cleared the camp, and were all mounted on horseback, Kanias led the twins through the trees to meet up with the white crushed rock trail that wound down the backside of the bluff, leading to a wide crease in the hills to either side. The weather was clear, the sun warm and comforting as it poked through the trees. It was nearly perfect traveling weather.

After an hour of meandering downhill, their course leveled and the trail widened. It took a straight course toward the gap between the hills. Kanias increased their pace to a brisk trot that the horses could easily sustain. The path was wide enough to be a road, so Raine and

Rennick flanked the Seraph making it easier for them talk and ride through the morning and into early afternoon. Kanias believed that at the rate they were traveling, with limited breaks, they would reach Jaske Green by nightfall. The promise of sleeping in a bed, eating warm food, and soaking in a hot bath was the best salve not just for achy muscles but for an injured ego.

Raine and Kanias imparted their bluff top conversation from earlier that morning to Rennick. Although it was not easy information to hear, it helped fill in some blanks from the previous day, details that they were first too frightened, and then too exhausted to share with Rennick the day before. Raine told him how during Jirri's Delving of her, the Seraph made a connection with the sole intention of breaking her mind, by revealing how she had murdered Dani.

Raine thoughtfully recalled the situation, her eyes darkening with each detail. "I learned that Dani was a Cou'Rali Adept and that she was not our real mother. But it was at the expense of watching her die as if I were there, all in just seconds. It was terrible."

Rennick was stunned. But his own shock was washed away by the rush of anguish and anger flowing out of his sister. His eyes darkened, as did Raine's, at the same speed and to the same degree.

Riding beside Rennick, Kanias nodded. "It's true. And Jair was Cou'Rali as well. I have never heard of two Adepts knowingly working together with a common Gran Shiga before." The Seraph shifted in his saddle before continuing. "I do not know how this whole puzzle fits together yet, but it is obvious to me that someone knew exactly who you both were and hid you in Domo Vale with the two best possible guardians." Kanias shook his head. "No one would have ever looked for Seraph in a Neph community, much less a Realmwalker. Whoever it was, they hid you in plain sight."

Rennick felt Raine grew more resolute as the conversation persisted. "Well, I intend on learning the truth," Raine said, her jaw clenched.

Rennick was thoughtful for a moment. "Kanias," he began, "If Jair and Dani are not our parents, who are? Where are they?"

Kanias simply shook his head. "If I knew, I would tell you," he said. "But the better question is who placed you in the care of two Cou'Rali

Adepts, making it their Gran Shiga? It ensured their commitment, but to what end? When those questions are answered, we will most likely know the identity of your birth parents." The Seraph frowned as he spoke. "You realize that had things gone differently yesterday, you would have been purified thus making you each useless as the Realmwalker or the Successor. Unless of course, that was the goal."

"Then there is the matter of Jirri and Tarien," Raine added. "And Red. After Jirri failed to break me, my Spirit took over and I had the feeling of complete authority over her."

"It is called *Aspect*," Kanias shared. "It is something that only Seraph can do. It is, in essence, revealing your Spirit form to another being." Kanias chuckled, "I am sure that your Aspect revealing itself as the Realmwalker within her mind was terrifying for her."

"She got what she deserved," Raine said flatly. "She had broken Tarien's mind at some point, and murdered Dani." She turned in her saddle to look directly at Kanias. "But as I told you this morning, Kanias, you were her target too. I know. I made her tell me. She was supposed to verify if one of us was the Realmwalker, then kill you and our entire family. Her plan was to frame us for your death."

Kanias smiled grimly. "I do not disagree with you, Raine, I just do not enjoy pondering the implications of what it means. At the very best, it suggests that two different groups with competing agendas knew exactly who you two were, where you were located, and who was protecting you."

Rennick's head was spinning, "And at the very worst?"

Kanias grimaced. "It means that some of the other Realms, if not all, are involved in a coordinated fashion."

"By the Goddess," breathed Rennick.

They rode on in silence. Rennick noticed that as they moved between the fir and oak-dotted slopes of the bluffs, Kanias was occasionally reaching out and feeling with the Lani. Rennick became more sensitive to what this felt like as his time with Kanias progressed. At first, he could only feel the Seraph pulling on what seemed like some invisible essence in the air. However, when they stopped for a quick break and a meal that afternoon, he was much more in tune with the process. Rennick could feel vague differences between the amount of Lani used, and when Kanias switched between them. Each Lani had its own distinct feeling, a vibration that he sensed deep within himself.

Rennick had many more questions for Kanias and Raine regarding everything that happened, but the Seraph's mood had soured, and he appeared to be satisfied with just riding in silence. Except to warn the twins of other travelers on the road as they appeared ahead or were about to pass them from behind, there was little talk at all. Whenever another rider appeared, Kanias instructed the twins to slow their horses, sit as tall as they could, and act polite but aloof. They were to give only a curt nod and avoid any direct eye contact. Kanias would carefully watch the behavior of anyone they met in order to determine whether they posed a legitimate threat to them.

Each occurrence passed without any incident, even as they grew closer to Jaske Green. As the bluffs began to fade into rolling hills and meadows, the traffic grew steadily. Area farmers pushing handcarts laden with produce and locals walking to the city joined the small ranks of random travelers they had been encountering for miles.

Despite the amount of movement and regardless of the number of those occupying the road, Rennick noticed that their path would open before the three of them only to close off quickly behind them as they moved through the street. It was as if the trio was encased in a bubble that floated its way along a river of live bodies. Most of the other travelers watched them in amazement, allowing the space around Raine, Rennick, and Kanias atop their horses to remain uniform and open. Many would bow, touching their heads in reverence. Some strayed near them, pleading for blessings from Erta, or making small supplications for assistance. But all gave way in the end. All were witness to the three Seraph. And all of them saw Raine.

Rennick watched his sister's posture remain straight, her elegant pose firmly fixed on back of the finely muscled brown mare. She did exactly as Kanias had instructed her to do, yet Rennick was in awe. His sister radiated confidence, authority, and power. Kanias and Rennick were likely her valets as far as the observers were concerned. The fact that they were even present was little more than a formality.

By the time they came over a rise in view of Jaske Green as it spread across the shallow valley below, the road ahead of them was abuzz with news of the coming Seraph.

So much for not calling attention to ourselves. We might as well have heralds and trumpets!

The bubble of space around them proceeded to carry the three down the road until it became caught in a current leading into the city. Masses of Jaske Green citizens flooded the street. Rennick looked to Kanias for direction, but only saw what had to be confusion on the Seraph's face. The situation was quite the opposite of what Kanias had hoped would occur, that is, three Seraph passing through town unnoticed. As indicated by the way that the people of Jaske Green were behaving, not only would they remember these Seraph, but they were certain to speak of one Seraph in particular—a long haired beauty— who arrived the day after Yelta Luna. And they would do so for many years to come.

Chapter 13: The Thunder Rolls

AS the crowd around Kanias, Rennick, and Raine grew more festive and boisterous, Rennick could see Kanias grow more nervous and agitated. The diverse mob of individuals that was at first quiet, respectful, and subdued, had now taken on enigmatic fervor. They reached out for Raine, calling to her even though they did not know her name. Those who saw her strained for a better view, to see more clearly something they did not understand. It was something of which they could not get enough. Everything about Raine—her beauty, her mystery, her very energy—was captivating if not consuming. They were insatiable.

Rennick had never seen anything like it before. He had seen young Neph in Domo Vale like Jenk Dakkon and Maret Standon, or even Garen Larnich the day before, moon over Raine, follow her around like pups, but what he was witness to at that moment was on a whole other scale. Old or young. Male or Female. Maior or Halen. Nym or D'ware. It did not matter. The masses had to see her. And when they did, they smiled. It could not be helped. He realized something very important there in the street. The dazed multitudes in awe of his sister were marking that point in their lives with that memory for a reason.

Rennick sensed his sister's initial shock at the outpour of attention. He thought this to be understandable, as he was also overwhelmed by the hum of the crowd and the fact that he had never seen so many in one place before in his life, certainly never in Domo Vale. After a moment however, and after the love for Raine became increasingly tangible, her eyes lightened and her demeanor relaxed. But her posture never faltered, and she never slumped in her saddle. It was obvious that she had begun to enjoy the attention, particularly when she saw the children craning necks and jumping for what could only be a glimpse of her.

As the crowd grew along with her ease in moving through it, however, Raine began noticing that the experience was having the opposite effect on Kanias. The uneasiness in the normally easy-going Seraph's manner was in his every gesture and breath. His usual sense of serenity was disappearing by the second. When Raine realized that Kanias had reached a point of desperate concern for their safety in what was an unpredictable situation, her eyes began to darken and Rennick could feel that she was becoming anxious as well.

They reached the outside of town and approached the point where the road split into a fork. One road descended into the center of the hamlet, while the other skirted around the north side of what was mostly a residential area. After leaving the village behind, the main street rejoined the road cutting through the middle of Jaske Green. From there it moved along the low hills and bluffs that spilled into the open grasslands of Rayvon.

Kanias was suspicious, looking at the center of the town as if it were a trap.

"What is it, Kanias?" Raine's voice was even and patient with the hope of not upsetting him anymore than he already was.

"We need food," he said, "And supplies." He looked at neither Raine nor Rennick when he spoke this. He just urged his horse forward in an attempt to turn north in order to bypass the center of town.

It occurred to Rennick that their food stores were limited. Kanias had said so when he'd given him the first little wax package of meat and cheese. The only supplies they had were what they took from the Pyn River camp. They need to find provisions at the first opportunity and reach the Temple as quickly as possible.

At first, the crowd simply resisted the trio's attempt to push themselves forward. As a result, their progress was merely slowed. But when the masses saw that the three had no intention of stopping, the bubble that had been a buffer of air between them and a multitude of arms began to shrink. Every hand reached for Raine. They jostled and pushed each other out of the way to get a better position. One by one, they squeezed between the three of them until Raine, Rennick, and Kanias were separated. The current of bodies on an odd river of worship was pulling them into Jaske Green.

Abruptly, and with force Rennick had not yet seen, Kanias stopped his horse and rose up in the stirrups. As the Seraph raised his hand into the air, the crowd fell silent, all faces turning to him to await the words of the emissary.

"Thank you for your welcome, residents and friends of Jaske Green!" Kanias voice was bright and loud. A few impromptu cheers rose as he spoke, but were quickly shushed. "Unfortunately," he continued. "We must press on tonight, as we are attending to an urgent matter in Cha'Li and cannot delay our arrival any further."

The cheers were now interspersed with shouts of *Who is she?* These were followed by cries of *Why is she here?* The crowd was eager to hear the answers to these questions and would not be swayed until they were satisfied.

Kanias was about to speak again. But the group was not pleased when they realized that it was the emissary they would hear and not Raine. Looking around, Raine rose up gracefully in her stirrups, raising both of her hands outward. She smiled. There was a roar of approval. Kanias was panic stricken, and looked at Raine as if he had never seen her before. He slowly sunk back into his saddle and waited for her to finish.

Rennick could feel the mixture of apprehension and exhilaration running through his sister, waving her arms once until everyone fell silent.

"Your curiosity honors me," she said in a loud and vibrant voice. Rennick felt his sister's confidence grow. Interestingly, he felt like one of the members of the throng around her. It was then that it became clear that he was not looking at his sister any more. He was in the presence of a young Realmwalker, one who was greeting and encouraging for the first time those she would be protecting. The citizens of Jaske Green gathered around her, representing every De'Lani in the Realm. They needed this moment. Raine could feel it. And she was going to give it to them.

"I am afraid that Seraph Kanias is correct, however, as I am needed for an urgent matter in Cha'Li." Her voice rang out like a bell over their heads. Then there was silence. The crowd awaited further instruction.

"But now that I have seen your charming village," she said. "I am certain to return soon." Raine bowed formally, bringing her hands to her head. "Thank you for allowing me to move along my way. May Erta's Blessing be upon you all."

Raine lowered herself back down into her saddle as the cheers and cries resumed. She beamed with pride and happiness watching the sea of faces open before an astonished Kanias. The Seraph nodded and clucked to his horse, leading Raine down out of the crowd and down the road, with Rennick trailing behind her. Rennick could feel the warmth radiate from his sister. It was as if she were in the orbit of her own sun.

No. Raine is the sun and everything will revolve around her.

The crowd filled in behind them, roaring after Raine as they left. Kanias picked up his pace and the twins followed until they finally cleared the last of the group of townsfolk. At last, they were able to transition into a gallop. Even as twilight fell around them, they rode at that speed until they were on the other side of a large hill heading into a thicket alongside the road. In the lead, Kanias slowed his horse to a walk and immediately upon entering the cover of the trees, rode north of the road, deeper into the thicket. Rennick could feel the Seraph using Lani power again, but this time he was using one and one alone.

After riding about one hundred strides, they came upon a small stream that cut into the hillside, emptying into a small pool in the meadow before it flowed downhill and away to the east. Kanias stopped his horse and directed the others to do so. After everyone had dismounted, the Seraph motioned for them to be silent. He continued to use his Lani power. It slowly grew in potency as he continued to use it.

His hands at his sides, feet hip distance apart, Kanias faced the east and closed his eyes. Moving then to the south, west, and then the north, the Seraph rotated clockwise in the span of about ten minutes. Then all of the sudden, his eyes snapped open. He looked to the both of them, first Rennick and then Raine.

"We are safe," he said. "No one has followed us." His smile was as large as it was genuine.

Rennick exchanged a puzzled look with Raine. Then they turned to the Seraph who was still smiling. There were tears in his eyes.

"When you stood up, Raine," Kanias said, "It was one of the most magnificent things I ever felt." Rennick had never seen Kanias so animated. He was gesturing with his hands and pacing back and forth as he continued. "I went from being fearful and frustrated to being completely at peace in just seconds."

Raine smiled. "I just thought that I had to give them what they wanted so they would let us leave."

"That is the thing," the Seraph replied. "You naturally know what people want and how to give it to them. I wanted a way out of the town without making the situation worse. You gave that to me. And of course the townspeople needed to feel like they were acknowledged and valued. You standing up accomplished both."

"Why did all of that happen?" Rennick chimed in. "I do not understand."

"It is the Aspect of the Realmwalker," Kanias responded. "That is the only explanation that I have. Raine has accepted it and it has become part of her. Part of what makes the Realmwalker powerful is his or her ability to relate to the needs of others."

"You sound surprised," said Raine. She looked at Kanias with a little grin.

"Honestly, Raine, I am," Kanias said. "It has been over a century since a Realmwalker roamed the Four Realms. Very few exist on Erta who truly know what it is like to be in the presence of one inhabited by the Aspect, so we know little about what to expect in real terms. We have our records and histories, but so often the true impact of physical experience is something that cannot be understood until it is witnessed firsthand, such as I did today."

It was growing dark in the thicket. As Kanias was talking, he collected some small twigs and short, dry limbs from around the clearing and placed them in an open area near the water's edge. He then reached into his pack and pulled out a firebrand. Igniting the tip, he applied it to the small pile he had prepared. It caught rapidly, spreading light throughout the small meadow and casting shadows on their faces.

Kanias directed the twins to set up a full camp, as they were well off the road, and he wanted to make sure that they received plenty of rest that evening. After providing the twins direction on setting up the camp, Kanias walked around and gathered more wood from the thicket. He returned to the fireside, gradually feeding the fire until it was tall and bright.

As Rennick busied himself with his assigned tasks, he observed Kanias. It was clear to him that today meant something to the burly Seraph. It could be as simple as that Kanias was proud of Raine. But Rennick was also proud. Who would not have been? But there was most likely something else driving the Seraph's pleasant disposition. When the thought came to Rennick, it seemed too simple to believe right away, but felt like the truth.

He is proud of himself!

As Rennick glanced over at Raine, he could see that she was smiling to herself as she unpacked her horse. But Rennick could feel his relief as if he had been holding his breath since breakfast. There was no question. He was glad it was over. As Raine spoke to the crowd today, Rennick began to view his sister from a completely different perspective. He had always believed she was amazing, and the simple fact that she was the Realmwalker would do nothing to change that. The truth was, however, that things had changed. And they were not going to change back.

Kanias was the one who had found the Realmwalker and the Successor, and after only one day, it was apparent that Raine was already changing the world for better. The Seraph could take pride in that it was he who had saved them, delivered them unto a waiting world, one hungry for what only a Realmwalker can provide. Hope.

Approaching each of the twins, Kanias checked their progress, smiled reassuringly, and returned to tending the fire and preparing food. The cooking tripod and the teapot already giving off its spicy, soothing scent, were in place over the fire. He had laid out a rough square of cloth and upon it had set cheese, cured meat, a small pile of hazelnuts, and the last six maoli. He then used the bag in which the food had been stored as a cushion for him.

Rennick had just finished unpacking his gear and rubbing down his horse when Raine appeared on the other side of Randor. He was not surprised when he glanced over his sister's shoulder to see that her chores were already finished. She smiled at him. He could feel that she was happy, calm, and content. Rennick smiled in return, but he was not quite as content as everyone else appeared to be. He still did not understand most of what was happening in their lives, but he was determined to get some answers. More had happened in past two days than had occurred in the twins' life. The excitement and frantic momentum had made it easy for Rennick to forget about a few things that were weighing on the back of his mind.

"Raine," Rennick started while he continued to unpack. "Do you believe all of this?"

Raine looked at him with a puzzled look. "Believe?" Her face had a flat affect. "Do you mean do I *believe* that two of the beings I loved most in the world are dead? Or do I *believe* that someone tried to kill you, the only one I have left?" Rennick fidgeted as he felt her irritation with the question. But Raine did not stop. "Or maybe you're wondering if I *believe* that I watched our village, the only home I've ever known, burn to the ground, likely because I simply exist?" Then she paused and looked at her brother with eyes as blue as they had been all day. "Or do you mean do I *believe* that I am the Realmwalker?"

Her eyes, still not darkening, bored into Rennick's. His were becoming black almost instantaneously.

"Yes, I believe all of those things," she said. "But If I believe the first few to be true, if I accept the despair that goes along with the tragedy of yesterday, then I have to accept the fact that I am the Realmwalker. If I do not, it means that there is no sense to it all, no reason, and that it was all for nothing." Raine eyed Kanias, who was busy laying out their dinner a few feet away.

"Maybe the only thing that matters at this point is if he believes in us," she said.

Rennick began to protest. "You mean you, you're the—,"

"No." Raine interrupted. "I mean us. This Seraph did not find The Realmwalker and her inadequate brother." Rennick smiled slightly but Raine continued in a very serious, straight forward tone. "He found The Realmwalker and The Successor. Erta needs us both, Rennick. She needs me and she needs you."

Rennick felt ashamed, a little awkward in fact. And perhaps more inadequate than ever. He had spent his entire life, and the last several days for that matter, believing that Raine was invincible. Rennick was always happy to follow in his sister's shadow. Now more than ever, her shadow was where he belonged, for Rennick was lost.

Raine was so certain of her direction, of where she would go and what she would do when she got there. Rennick had trouble placing one foot in front of the other without falling down. He did not know what he was supposed to do or what was expected of him in light of his new role. Unlike his sister, he certainly was not able to *feel* what people needed, often before they themselves knew they were missing anything. Rennick needed training at every level. His impromptu lesson with the sword earlier that morning with Kanias proved that.

Raine walked around the horse that was standing between her and her brother. She ran her hand over the horse's hind end and over its left flank, immediately putting it at ease. She placed her arm around Rennick's shoulder. He felt a similar sense of calm.

"I need you, Rennick," she said. She was not looking at him but he could feel her eyes lighten, blooming into a shade blue that was almost gray. "You are more than my brother. You are my security, and my protector. No one can help me as you can, because no one understands me, or knows what I am feeling and thinking like you do. After all that has happened in the last day, I need to know that there is still one constant in this world. And that is you."

"She is right, Successor," said Kanias, his voice shattering the night air.

The twins turned toward the Seraph. Kanias did not say anything more, instead just gesturing to the clearing where the fire was a few feet away. Raine and Rennick walked to where the cloth lay, sitting next to one another on one side of it. The Seraph followed, sitting across from them, immediately passing the food items around. Within a few moments, their meat and cheese rations were gone and they were enjoying their tea with the last of the maoli—two apiece.

After they had each eaten their fill, they lay on their backs and watched the sky lighten as the sun made its trip back to Natura's sky. For a few moments, the world outside of the thicket had ceased to exist. Chatting and smiling as if they were children, they went on about things that had nothing to do with the last several days. Rennick enjoyed every moment. Kanias was telling them stories of when he was in training as Seraph initiate years before. It was odd, hearing stories of his education, at sometimes not succeeding at the tasks placed before him. Rennick had always lived with the assumption that Seraph were infallible, nearly perfect beings. Although he had never met a Seraph before Kanias, with the exception of Tarien and Jirri, he had an idea of what they were like. Their reputation had become their myth. But Kanias seemed genuine and willing to accept that he was no better than any other being. For Rennick, it was safe to assume that most Seraph were not like Kanias.

Rennick was feeling better now, but he still had questions. The one that had bothered him the most was something that Jair had said to him.

Beware of the Shadowman.

Propping himself up on one elbow, he looked over at Kanias. The Seraph saw his movement and turned to look back at him. "Is something on your mind, Rennick?"

For some reason, Rennick was hesitant in mentioning the name or title, but he ventured the question anyhow.

"Who is the Shadowman?" Rennick did not realize how terrifying the image in his head was until he illustrated the image with his voice.

The Seraph's face dropped a little, but it brightened up with a chuckle and nod, "Now you want to tell ghost stories?"

"No," Rennick replied. "One of the last things Jair said to me was 'Beware of the Shadowman.' I had hoped that you would know what it meant."

What was a falsely hopeful smile dissolved from Kanias' face. He rolled over onto his back and laced his fingers behind his head. The Seraph didn't look at Rennick but his concentration toward him was so intense that it did not make much difference.

"Tell me everything that he told you," he said. "Everything." Kanias exhaled the breath in his body to the point that Rennick heard the Seraph's chest rattle. He watched Raine sit up, straight-backed and listen as Rennick told them about the Sending from Jair after being impaled upon the beam.

There was a long pause after Rennick finished speaking. He could feel the fear and confusion coming from Raine, and the concern in the way Kanias tensed every muscle in his body.

"What is wrong?" Rennick asked.

Kanias rolled onto his side and poked the fire with a long stick, the flames outlining the worry so apparent on his face.

"Shadowman is the name of a real being that has become so shrouded in myth, that it is difficult to tell what is real and what is not," he said. "He is not of this Realm, but it is said that he travels between them, leaving death in his wake."

Sitting up and leaning in toward the fire, Kanias looked at the twins. "Again, most of the stories are likely to greatly exaggerate the abilities and motives of the Shadowman, but I will not ruin a good night's sleep by telling you more tonight. I need to consider a few things, and then we will talk more in the morning." Kanias smiled, and tried to hide the cloud of worry behind his eyes.

That night, Rennick had a difficult time sleeping. His mind was churning with every new danger he had encountered of late.

Cou'Rali. Shadowman. Fire-hurling beings. The Seraph divided. RED. All around us—questions and threats. I failed against Tarien, I failed against Kanias. How am I to help or protect Raine when I cannot even defend myself against a single foe, one at a time? I need to learn and now! Raine is depending on me—

Rennick was standing in the clearing at the top of the bluff in the Domo Hills. Low dense clouds and the distant roll of thunder announced a coming storm. The wind blowing through the trees around the clearing sent cascades of leaves swirling around him in a gentle cyclone of brown and yellow. Rennick felt something heavy in his right hand and recognized the weight of it as Jair's sword. He looked down to see the bright blue of the sapphire beckoning him like water would if he were dying of thirst. Raising the sword, he wondered how he was holding it when he was certain that he left it bundled in his gear by the horses.

He looked up from the sword, and saw someone across the clearing. Raine. She was walking toward him, her chestnut hair whipping in the wind behind her. She smiled and waved at her brother, as she often did. He was about to return the gesture, when he heard the roll of thunder again, a prelude for the appearance of a dark figure peeking out from around the tree behind Raine.

"Raine," he yelled above the thunder. He ran toward her, hoping that he would be fast enough. He had to reach her before the dark figure did.

Rennick had run only five strides when the dark figure burst from under the shadows of the trees, revealing Tarien's burned and disfigured body. A thin, cold smile framed his teeth, causing the torn and charred skin to crack and peel away from his lips and cheeks, making the unemotional Seraph appear beyond terrifying. The skeletal Seraph, covered in gashes and burns became a blur. Before Rennick could move to catch his sister, Tarien had her in a headlock once again, holding his knife against her neck, a small line of blood trickling down where the blade had nicked her. He looked at Rennick's sword and laughed. Rennick looked down at his own hand to see his small hunting knife there instead of the sword.

Rennick had been here before.

"Tarien!"

A deep rumble of thunder poured over him as Raine screamed while Tarien drew the blade across her neck, a thick curtain of blood pouring out of the slit. He let her go and she crumpled to the ground, landing in the blood soaked earth at her feet. The storm was on top of them now, and the thunder was a constant rumble that shook the ground beneath their feet. As he leapt to Raine's side, she looked up at him with accusing eyes.

"Why didn't you protect me?"

The thunder continued to roll, and Rennick heard himself scream.

TO BE CONTINUED:

The Realmwalker Chronicles:
The Pillars of Natura
Volume 2: Halen

CPSIA information can be obtained at www.ICGtesting.com
Printed in the USA
LVOW10s1953140415

434584LV00014B/30/P

9 780986 360114